AGAIN
AGAIN

e. lockhart

HOT
KEY
BOOKS

First published in Great Britain in 2020 by
HOT KEY BOOKS
80–81 Wimpole St, London W1G 9RE
www.hotkeybooks.com

A CIP catalogue record for this book is available from the British Library.

ISBN: 978-1-4714-0792-1
Also available as an ebook and in audio

1

This book is typeset in 10.5pt Berling
Interior design by Trish Parcell and Perfect Bound Ltd

Printed and bound in Great Britain by Clays Ltd, Elcograf S.p.A.

Hot Key Books is an imprint of Bonnier Books UK
www.bonnierbooks.co.uk

For Daniel

CONTENTS

PART I

PART II

AGAIN
AGAIN

PART I

1

A LOVE STORY

This story takes place in a number of worlds.
But mostly in two.

It was the third day of Adelaide Buchwald's summer job, the
summer after her junior year at boarding school.

That summer she would fall in and out of love more than
once,

in different ways

in different possible worlds.

In every world, she was consumed with the intense
contradictions of her heart.

Adelaide wanted to be rescued and

she wanted independence.

She was inclined to laziness,

curiosity, and

magical thinking.

She was all charm and yet deeply miserable. She was a liar
and she hated liars. She loved both truly and wrongheadedly.
She appreciated beauty.

3

Her job was to walk five dogs, morning and night. They belonged to teachers who were on summer vacation.

EllaBella,

Lord Voldemort,

Rabbit,

Pretzel, and

the Great God Pan.

Those were the dogs. The morning she met Jack, Adelaide took them all to the dog run on the Alabaster Preparatory Academy campus. The run was a sandy space, fenced in and surrounded by trees. Looking through the leaves, she could see the spire of the Alabaster clock tower. She unleashed the dogs and sat on a bench while they frolicked. She listened to podcasts about stupid celebrities she didn't even care about, trying to stop thinking about Mikey Double L.

Adelaide threw balls for the dogs. She threw sticks. She collected poop in small plastic bags, then threw them in the trash.

EllaBella said, *You're a gentle human. Can I lean on you?* And Adelaide let the dog lean. She stroked EllaBella's shaggy head.

She texted her mom about the breakup with Mikey. She had already told her dad the little she thought he needed to know.

Adelaide and her father, Levi Buchwald, had moved to Alabaster Prep for her junior year of high school. Adelaide lived in a dormitory, and Levi in Alabaster faculty housing. His new home was a small wooden house on the edge of campus. It was furnished with flea-market buys and overloaded with books. He was an English teacher.

Adelaide's mother, Rebecca, and her little brother, Toby, had spent the year together in a rental house in Baltimore. Toby was very sick. Rebecca was taking care of him.

Rebecca was a knitter. She used to own a store called the Good Sheep Yarn Shop, where she taught classes. Much of her home was dedicated to wicker baskets overflowing with skeins of yarn. And plants, which she tended semi-obsessively. Rebecca was a person who focused very intently on the people, plants, and yarn in front of her.

She texted Adelaide back immediately about Mikey:

Oh blergh. I'm sorry. You okay?

Adelaide lied.

Yeah.

What happened?

The last thing Adelaide wanted to do was tell her mother the story of Mikey Double L.

. . .

. . .

Well, I'm here if you want
to talk. Hug! 🖤 🖤 🐳 .

Rebecca often used the fat, spouting whale emoji. Adelaide had no idea what it was meant to symbolize. She wrote back.

5

Breakup was probably for the
best anyway.

I was sad. But I slept it off and
had eggs for breakfast, and
now I'm feeling much better.

You're very mature. 🐋 🐋 🐋

Adelaide was not at all mature. And the breakup wasn't for the
best. But she didn't want her mother to spiral into anxiety. That
was something Rebecca was inclined to do, with Adelaide off
at boarding school. She wanted to hear that Adelaide ate well,
stayed hydrated, got regular exercise, and slept enough.

When Rebecca spiraled into worry, the result was a series
of phone calls filled with urgent requests for reassurance and
connection that ended in Adelaide yelling at her mother, so
Adelaide had devised a plan of regular texts giving evidence of
those desirable behaviors.

"But I slept it off and had eggs for breakfast, and now I'm
feeling much better" was what Rebecca needed to hear. Not
"I'm puffy and dehydrated from crying and
for breakfast I ate two Hershey bars and
truthfully I feel
unlovable
and ugly,
stupid
and broken.

I wish I could get a giant injection that would turn off my thoughts.

I would let a creepy doctor with a secret basement lab shoot a

random glowing substance into my ear if I knew it would stop me from feeling the way I do.

Last night, I tried binge-watching baking shows and then

I tried binge-watching zombie shows and then

I tried listening to happy music and

putting on a ton of makeup. So much makeup. Then my eyebrows (with their makeup) looked scary and

their scariness made me depressed.

I was depressed by my own eyebrows.

I would have tried smoking cigarettes if I'd had any, and

I would have drunk Dad's booze if he had any, but no luck on mind-altering substances, so

I passed out at three a.m. and when I woke up

I felt even worse and

my pillowcase was stained with lipstick."

No. She couldn't say that to her mother.

Adelaide just sent the text about the good breakfast and the night's sleep. She added a zebra emoji for good measure, thinking Rebecca would like it. Then she put her phone in her pocket.

The Great God Pan lay on the ground, releasing gas.

EllaBella stayed close, pressing against Adelaide's leg. *I am thinking you have dog treats in your pocket*, she said sweetly.

Lord Voldemort and Pretzel played chase. Rabbit growled at something on the other side of the fence.

And suddenly, a boy appeared. He was already in the run

when Adelaide saw him, standing under a tree. He had a fluffy white dog on a leash.

Adelaide recognized the dog. It was B-Cake. B-Cake belonged to Sunny Kaspian-Lee.

A beat later, Adelaide recognized the boy as well, though she was sure she'd never seen him at Alabaster. He had a sweet V-shaped face and full lips. He was broad in the shoulders, with a narrow nose, smooth-shaven face, delicate ears. His light brown hair was wavy and a little wild. He was the sort of person you'd see immortalized in Roman statuary, his skin a warm Mediterranean olive, his chin and neck strong. He wore a light cotton jacket, a blue T-shirt, loose jeans, and green suede sneakers with blue stripes. The sleeves of the jacket were rolled up. His hands had the slight squashy look of leftover baby fat.

She knew him. She was certain of it.

He nodded at her, walked over, and draped himself onto the bench. There was something unusual going on with one of his legs. He walked with a roll of his left hip, and the fabric of his jeans flapped around that leg.

She remembered his walk.

The boy released the clip on the leash. B-Cake zoomed over to Rabbit and Rabbit exploded into the air with an anxious yip.

The boy laughed, covering his mouth with his fist. "Poor puppy," he said.

"Hey, do I remember you?" she asked.

"Me? I don't know."

"I'm pretty sure I *do* remember you," she said. "From Boston. Two years ago. We met at a rooftop party when I was in ninth grade."

"A party on whose rooftop?"

"I don't know. A friend of my friend. It was cold and you let me wear your scarf. Remember?"

The boy shook his head. "I have a radically terrible memory. Sorry." Then he took out his phone. "'Scuse me, I've got to make a call."

"Hey, do I remember you?" Adelaide asked.

"Me?" he said. "I don't know."

"I'm pretty sure I *do* remember you," she said. "From Boston."

"I've never been to Boston," he said.

"Hey, do I remember you?" Adelaide asked.

"Me? I don't know."

"I'm pretty sure I *do* remember you," she said. "I'm

pretty sure, in fact, that you took my number at a party two years ago and

you never, ever texted me, is what I'm

pretty sure of. I'm

pretty sure you're the kind of terrible human being who says

9

Give me your number

when he doesn't actually want the number, and I'm

pretty sure that's not the kind of human being I need to
talk to ever again,

especially not right now, when Mikey Double L is off to
Puerto Rico full of virtue and

my entire sense of myself is

quite frankly

on the verge of liquidation."

"Okay then," he said. "I don't need to make conversation."

"I'm pretty sure I *do* remember you," Adelaide said. "From
Boston. Two years ago. We met at a rooftop party."

"Really?"

"You were writing in a notebook," she explained. "We started
talking."

"What was I writing?"

Adelaide flushed. She

wanted to tell the boy the answer, and also, she

didn't want to tell him.

"We talked about dinosaurs, I think, and which ones we'd
like to turn into."

"Velociraptor, obviously," said the boy.

"That's what you said, but you're one hundred percent
wrong," said Adelaide. "Pterodactyl."

"Oh, you're right," he said. "Pterodactyl is better. Flight is
always better."

"I used to have a fear of plesiosaurs," she told him. "Do you know about plesiosaurs? They were like, giant naked turtles with sea-monster necks."

He laughed.

"At the rooftop party, you gave me your scarf," continued Adelaide. "A red and black one. You said I could use it but to give it back, because it wasn't even yours, it was your cousin's."

"Was I wearing a terrible leather jacket? Like a trying-too-hard jacket?"

"Yes."

"Then it was me," he said. "But I can't remember."

"My ride was leaving and I gave the scarf back to you, and you ripped a page from your notebook. You gave me the page and you had written me a poem:

> *Cerulean dress and*
> *wide eyes, like a lion.*
> *A raging wave of disobedient hair.*
> *She contains*
> *contradictions."*

"I wrote you a poem?"

"You did."

Adelaide was sad he didn't remember. Maybe he gave poems to a lot of girls. Or maybe he just couldn't be expected to recall a party from two and a half years ago, when they would both have been only fourteen.

"I think poems, sometimes," she told him. "Often, actually. But I rarely write them down."

"Do you still have the one I wrote you?" he asked.

It was in her wallet. "Maybe somewhere," she told him.

Adelaide had asked people if they knew a boy of his description, a boy with a roll of his hip, a poet, a boy with soft-looking wrists and golden skin and bitten nails. She had looked for him again and again as she sat in coffeehouses, as she waited in line for a burrito. At parties or ramen places, she looked for his sweet, full mouth. She was holding on to the chance that something good might happen.

To Adelaide, the boy was a promise. He promised her that happiness could still exist,

could still be hers.

And that promise seemed even more important once the bad stuff started happening with Toby.

Then the Buchwald family left Boston. They moved to Baltimore for Toby's treatment. Adelaide had accepted that she'd never see the boy in the leather jacket, ever again.

Now here he was.

He picked up a tennis ball that was lying in the sand. "Birthday! Come here, boy."

"She's a girl," Adelaide said.

"Come here, girl."

B-Cake ignored him.

"She doesn't fetch," Adelaide told him. "I know that dog."

The boy laughed. "Okay. I don't need to throw if she's not into it." He sat down.

"Did you hurt your leg?" Adelaide asked.

"No." He didn't speak for a moment. Then he said, "Actually, a plesiosaur bit me. I didn't want to tell you because you seem to have a phobia."

"Ha." She chewed her lip. "Was that rude of me, asking?"

"A little." He sighed. "I was born this way. It's a skeletal limb abnormality."

"I'm sorry. I asked without thinking."

"You're not entitled to the knowledge, is all. It's my personal info. You know?"

"Okay."

"Okay."

"D'you want to ask me something intrusive now?" she said. "You can. I feel I owe you."

"No thanks."

"Ask me."

"That's all right."

"Go on."

"Fine. Ah, besides plesiosaurs, what scares you the most? Really, truly terrifies you?"

"My brother," Adelaide said, the answer coming out before she had time to craft an amusing reply.

He picked up a tennis ball that was lying in the sand. "Birthday! Come here, boy."

"She's a girl," Adelaide said.

"Come here, girl."

B-Cake ignored him.

"She doesn't fetch," Adelaide told him. "I know that dog."

The boy laughed. "Okay. I don't need to throw if she's not into it." He sat down next to her. "I'm just taking her this weekend while the owner's out of town. Are all of these yours?" He was talking about EllaBella, Rabbit, and the rest.

"I just walk them."

He reached down to pet EllaBella, who was lying at Adelaide's feet. "This dog is my favorite," he said. "She has an excellent beard." EllaBella was a bushy black mutt, nearly fifteen years old.

"She's my favorite too," Adelaide whispered. "But don't tell the others."

EllaBella was owned by Derrick Byrd, a single teacher of history. He'd come to Alabaster last year. He still had unpacked boxes in his house, which was two doors down from her dad's.

"I never tell secrets," said the boy. She liked the way his mouth moved when he spoke. He had blue paint underneath his nails.

"What did you paint?" she asked.

"I have access to the art studio for the summer. I'm painting abstract shapes, I guess you'd call them. Things that look like other things but aren't those things."

"Like what?"

"This one I'm doing—don't laugh."

"I won't."

"Well, you can laugh. It's kind of a hippopotamus and it's kind of a car. And also, it's kind of a church. The meaning is what the viewer sees in it."

14

"Hm."

"I'm not getting the effect I want," he said. "A lot of them look like blobs, not church hippos or whatever. It's just the start of an idea."

"What year are you?" she asked.

"Rising senior."

"I've never seen you. On campus."

He told her he had just transferred in. "My mother died six months ago." She'd had leukemia. He and his father had just relocated from Spain. His dad used to teach at Alabaster and was now going to head the Modern Languages department.

"I'm so sorry," Adelaide said. "About your mother."

"Yeah, well. Thanks." Lord Voldemort came up and wagged his stubby tail. "How come you walk so many dogs?"

"The teachers go away on summer travel. My father teaches English, but this summer he's working in Admissions for extra money. I got the idea to collect people's dogs and take them out, morning and evening. I feed them, too."

"I'm gonna get Birthday to fetch," he said. "Watch me."

He chased after B-Cake, showing her the tennis ball. "You know you want it. Look at it, so yellow. Covered with awesome dog slime. Watch it, watch it!"

B-Cake ignored him. Finally, Pretzel leaped up and grabbed the tennis ball from the boy's hand, then took it off to a corner to enjoy.

Adelaide smiled for the first time since Mikey had broken up with her.

"What are their names?" the boy asked.

"The big black one is EllaBella. The small hairy one who took the tennis ball is Pretzel. The pit bull is Rabbit."

"Aren't pit bulls vicious?"

"They have a strong bite, but nah. If they're treated well, they have good personalities."

"Wait, isn't this one a pit bull too?" He pointed.

"Nuh-uh. The Great God Pan is a French bulldog."

"And that one?"

"Lord Voldemort is a bull terrier."

He shrugged. "Variations on a theme. Same basic thing."

"You said something similar when we met at the rooftop party."

He shook his head, not remembering.

"You said," explained Adelaide, "that all the roof parties were variations on a theme. You said the parties echoed each other. Warm summer nights, drinks in plastic washtubs and people in shorts. The same songs playing."

Remember me, she willed him.

Remember the party. And the poem.

Remember what you said. Then remember what I said.

"That dog is trying to jump the fence," the boy announced.

Adelaide looked.

Rabbit the pit bull was crouched, waggling her back end like a cat about to spring.

"She can't go over," Adelaide said.

"She's trying. Look at her try."

And Rabbit jumped.

Rabbit was burly and dark gray, with a white chest and white paws. Her mouth was that wide pit-bull mouth that looks like a smile, and her legs were short and stocky. Her neck was so thick it could not properly be called a neck at all.

She cleared the fence.

In a hot second she was followed by B-Cake. It defied the laws of physics.

Adelaide took a run at the fence and jumped herself over. The boy came out through the gate holding the leash. "Birthday! Come here, Birthday!" he called.

B-Cake and Rabbit were tumbling on the lawn, running in manic circles.

"She goes by B-Cake," Adelaide informed him, stopping her chase to rest. "Not Birthday. She won't even know Birthday is her name."

"Why wouldn't Kaspian-Lee tell me that?" the boy moaned.

Sunny Kaspian-Lee was Adelaide's teacher. She taught Design for the Theater, which was a class on costumes, props, and lighting. And Set Design. Adelaide had taken them both.

When they ran into each other on campus, Kaspian-Lee always said "Hello, Adelaide Buchwald," and Adelaide always said "Hello, Ms. Kaspian-Lee." The teacher wore sculptural clothes and had short bangs that stopped midway down her forehead. In cold weather, she'd be wrapped in a burgundy trench coat, with a black watch cap, walking B-Cake to and from the Arts Center. She often carried unwieldy bags full of poster boards, long wooden dowels, and once, feathers. She would hold them against her torso with both arms, with B-Cake's leash hooked around one wrist.

Now, as the dogs raced and tumbled over each other, Adelaide chased Rabbit. The boy threw himself across the grass to tackle B-Cake. He missed her, though, and she ran past him.

"She'll murder me if I lose her dog," he said, scrambling to his feet.

Adelaide took a dog biscuit out of her jacket pocket and whistled.

B-Cake and Rabbit ran over.

"Sit," Adelaide commanded.

B-Cake sat. Rabbit didn't sit.

Adelaide took a second biscuit out and held it up. "There's one for each of you. Sit."

The boy snapped the leash onto B-Cake. He bent down and took hold of Rabbit's collar.

Adelaide gave each dog a biscuit. They took the treats gingerly, being careful not to hurt her with their fangs.

"I like that you have dog biscuits in your pockets," said the boy. "It takes a certain kind of person to always be prepared with a treat."

Adelaide *was* the type to have biscuits in her pocket, and gum in her backpack, and ChapStick, and hand cream that smelled like apricots. That morning she had coffee with three sugars in a thermos. "I carry a *lot* of treats," she told him as they returned to the dog run. She pulled some warm toast, wrapped in foil, out her bag. "Want some?"

"What is it?" He bent over and smelled.

"Rye toast. With butter."

"I've never had rye."

"It's good. I mean, it's not bacon. But nothing's bacon." She handed him a piece and he ate it thoughtfully.

18

"My name is Adelaide, by the way."

"Jack."

She already knew his name. From the party. "Why are you walking B-Cake?" she asked.

"Kaspian-Lee went off for the weekend with Mr. Schlegel," he said. "She asked me to walk the dog. Did you know they're *lovers*?" He emphasized the word.

"I knew they were a couple. They've been to my dad's for dinner."

"She used that word. *Lovers.*"

"Ew." They were quiet for a moment. Jack stood up. His mood seemed to have shifted. His eyes didn't meet hers. "I appreciate you saving me with dog biscuits," he said.

"Can I text you sometime?" Adelaide asked.

He shook his head. "I would say yes, but I'm super busy this summer. See you around, Adelaide. Fun chat."

Adelaide gave up on Rabbit and tackled B-Cake, rolling in the grass as the dog scrabbled with her paws. She hugged B-Cake to her chest.

Are we wrestling? asked B-Cake, switching immediately from recalcitrant to licky.

"Oh god, she's slobbering me," Adelaide called.

The boy loped over and bent to clip the leash on, but Rabbit had circled back and B-Cake lunged, pulling him as she leaped away. He kept hold of the dog but fell to the ground next to Adelaide.

Pushing herself up, Adelaide managed to grab Rabbit's collar as she ran by. "These are rotten dogs," she said. "You're rotten dogs, did you know that?"

They didn't know. They loved themselves.

Adelaide took firm hold of Rabbit's collar, pulled the leash out of her pocket, and clipped it on. Rabbit grumbled, but Adelaide ignored her and lay back in the grass to catch her breath.

Jack lay back as well. His shirt rode up, and Adelaide could see a thick, puckered scar on one side of his abdomen. His ordinary skin looked unbelievably soft and vulnerable next to the wound.

"Well, that was a thrill," he said. "Good catch, there."

"Yeah, well," she said. "I am a professional dog walker."

He laughed and stood up, making his scar disappear.

He held his hand out to her. She took it and he pulled her up. His hand was warm and she wanted to touch him more, wanted to run her finger up his arm.

But he let go. "Thanks for the B-Cake capture," he said. "I should get her back home before something worse happens."

That was so fun, said B-Cake. *Rabbit is my best friend.*

"Will you be here tomorrow, then?" Adelaide asked.

"I might be."

"I'm here all summer," Adelaide said.

He smiled. She told him her phone number and he texted her, "Hello."

Then he disappeared down the path.

A moment later, he returned with a reluctant B-Cake under his arm. "Adelaide with the cerulean dress," he called. "I remember now.

Cerulean dress and
wide eyes, like a lion.
A raging wave of disobedient hair."

And with that recitation, Adelaide Buchwald gave Jack Cavallero her heart.

Impulsively,

gloriously,

openly,

she gave it to him, falling in love with someone she did not know, wondering at the curve of his cheek, and the wave of his hair, and the way his shirt draped over his shoulders.

He made her laugh. He dared to write poems. He risked looking foolish in order to create something beautiful or strange.

She wanted to know the story of the scar on his abdomen. How had he gotten that wound? How well had it healed?

She could see by looking at him that he had been

vulnerable.

That he had

lived.

Survived.

She wanted to see all his scars, see all of him, and she felt

suddenly,

intensely

certain

that he was a safe person to show her own scars to.

She thought, *Maybe we have known each other always. Maybe our hearts encountered each other somehow,*

like two hundred years ago at a cotillion, with him in a frock

coat and me in whatever, some kind of elegant and complicated
dress.

    Or maybe our encounter was in another
possible world. That is,
in one of the countless other versions of this universe, the
worlds running parallel to this one,
we are already
in love.

2

THE WEIRD GRANDIOSITY
OF THE HUMAN MIND

Alabaster Preparatory Academy is a boarding school. It is the sort of place that offers classes like Eastern Religions, Theories of Popular Culture, and Microeconomic Theory. Students play lacrosse and row crew. They live in quaint residence halls that smell of wood and have no elevators. There is a chapel with large stained-glass windows. Most of the buildings are gray stone. There are woods on one side of the campus, and there's a small town on the other.

The place is full of fairly smart, mostly moneyed kids, largely Protestant, largely white. As such, its history and biases are worthy of some interrogation, which shall not be done thoroughly here, but which has been done elsewhere, you can be sure.

In recent years the student body has become more socially active, and more diverse. Protest posters decorated the dormitory hallways, speaking out against voter suppression, in support of gun control laws and gender-neutral bathrooms. The cafeteria had a well-stocked salad bar and gluten-free options. There were multiple student affinity groups.

Still, the place smelled of old money. And a century of male dominance.

As a middle-class white Jewish "faculty brat" with a public school background, Adelaide was conscious of both fitting in and not fitting in.

Levi Buchwald, Adelaide's father, had loved teaching public school. He got all passionate about pedagogical methods and presented his ideas at conferences. But when the family moved to Baltimore for Toby's treatment, he had been hard-pressed to find a job. It was the middle of the school year. Nobody was hiring. And even for positions that would start in the fall, there were very few openings. Eventually he applied to teach at Alabaster, where an old colleague was head of the English department.

He got the job and it paid reassuringly well, more than he'd made before, which was needed, since Rebecca was focused on Toby and managing his care. Levi's children could go to Alabaster for much-reduced tuition, so he and Adelaide had moved in late August, leaving Toby and Rebecca in Baltimore.

Adelaide lived in the dorms during the school year, but now, during the summer, she'd be with Levi in his two-bedroom house, sleeping in what was usually his office.

Adelaide's experience at Alabaster had been all right. Good, in a number of ways, though disastrous in one. She marveled at the bright green of the lawns, the stone buildings, the cobblestone paths. The Alabaster students were sporty and arty and often lax about their homework in a way she found endearing. They forgot their binders or lost their books. They carried everything from building to building in enormous backpacks, never even thinking about using the lockers they supposedly had combinations to. Their clothing seemed to be at its peak of fashion when threadbare. Girls wore ancient jeans, scuffed winter boots, and T-shirts that looked handed down generations, loose at the neck.

The disaster was that because of the terrible stuff going on with Toby, Adelaide dreamed of him at night, bad dreams about Toby's

babyish white tube socks, his

lime-green toothbrush, his

bluish mouth, and his

wheezy breath,

dreams where the only noise was that

sad, fragile Toby breath, wheezing, louder and louder.

Adelaide would wake up sweating.

And because her sleep was terrible and also because of the massive distraction

of falling deeply and head-spinningly in love with Mikey Double L,

Adelaide did not do her schoolwork.

Alabaster was significantly more challenging than either of her previous high schools. She turned in papers that would have been deemed strong back in Baltimore, only to have them handed back as unacceptable. Science labs went okay, and she caught up in math, but she found herself unable to force herself to rework the already-written papers. She didn't really understand what was wrong with them, and diving back in meant she

25

had to relive the humiliation of having done badly. Plus Mikey Double L was around, texting "Come to my fencing match? 3 pm," or "Let's get pizza off campus," or "There's nobody in my suite for the next hour and I wish you were here please please please come see me please love Mikey."

Mikey's work came easy for him, and Adelaide didn't want to tell him she had failed multiple essays. And her roommate/best friend, Stacey S, worked incredibly hard. Adelaide didn't want to tell her about slacking off. Stacey could be very judgy.

In the end, Adelaide was put on academic probation for spring term, which meant she had to get her marks up or be kicked out, basically.

But spring term, things were even worse with Toby. Adelaide's sleep got worse, too, and her relationship with Mikey was more intense than ever.

Although Levi sat down with her to go over her English papers, she still got a D in Global Studies for handing in half-finished work or no work at all. She flat-out failed the Set Design class. She just didn't do the final project, which was building a model.

Every day, she told herself she'd start work on it.

Every day, she felt overwhelmed. Or

ashamed. Or

she let herself be distracted by Mikey, by

a Lego diorama she was building, or by

Stacey S, who had interesting romantic entanglements and fashion questions.

It didn't help that you were supposed to build your set model in Kaspian-Lee's studio classroom, where all the supplies were.

When Adelaide went in there, people were putting finishing touches on their projects, while she hadn't even started. And when the

shame washed over her, she responded by

sparkling. She had, for example, talked at length to Mikey's suitemate Aldrich Nguyen, a pimply fencer whose design was both wobbly and frankly half-assed but was nearly finished. She distracted Aldrich for twenty minutes, convincing him to come to the vending machines with her, making jokes, using the photocopier to make pictures of her face and suggesting he use the copies as wallpaper for his design.

But when she sat down to attempt work, back came the shame, filling the room like smoke, and Adelaide's impulse was to flee. She went to see Mikey, who made her feel beautiful and clever.

Adelaide knew she was wasting this super-fancy education, at least in part, and she knew she was messing up the grades she needed to get into college, but she did not know how to make herself do anything different. The pull of distraction, and distraction by Mikey in particular, was irresistible.

Her favorite part of being a student at Alabaster was the Factory Center for Contemporary Arts. The Factory was technically one town over from Alabaster, a twenty-minute bike ride away. Students could sign out of campus and visit the museum for free. The art history and studio art classes were always going there.

It was built on the grounds of what used to be a paper mill and only featured art made by living artists. Most of it was extremely weird. You entered through an imposing iron gate, and once you were inside, there was a group of mammoth brick buildings. Most of the grounds were concrete, with sculptures scattered about.

Adelaide loved the Factory's large artificial spaces. They tapped something in her. When she stood in those rooms, her world

expanded. Beyond

Toby's illness and

Mikey's sweetness, beyond

her classes and her family.

She felt awe. That's what it was. Human beings were capable of

creating beauty and strangeness far beyond what nature offered. Their minds could be

weird and grandiose. They could conceive of

more than what was in front of them,

more than facts they'd learned.

Example: An exhibit of dioramas, each about the size of a couch. Each glass diorama box contained a silver mobile home. Underneath the mobile homes, you saw the earth in a cross-section.

Look closely, and in that earth, you saw a rabbit's burrow and the roots of trees.

There were worms in the dirt.

In one diorama, the earth hid a dinosaur skeleton.

In another, a dead body.

The artist's name was Teagan Rabinowitz.

Adelaide left that room feeling different about her feet on the ground.

Another example: A room of skeletons. They were bone white and displayed like exhibits in a natural history museum. But they were the skeletons of monsters. There was a minotaur. A griffin. Two dragons. A three-headed dog.

Alongside each one was a card. The one next to the griffin read "Unearthed in a tar pit outside San Diego, California, in 1952 by Gerald Booker and his archeological team. Estimated date of death: 1451. Note the incomplete left wing."

The art was attributed to the Society for the Excavation and Preservation of Biological Wonders.

The exhibit gave Adelaide a thrill. *Maybe such things are real.*

There's no proof they aren't.

3

A PHILOSOPHICAL PARTY

After Jack left the dog run, Adelaide went home and took a shower. She went grocery shopping in her father's car. Unloading everything into the fridge, she made herself two sandwiches of toasted bread and strawberry jam. She drank a can of seltzer.

Then she looked for Jack. She collected EllaBella from Byrd's house and walked the old dog around, hopeful of running into him. The Alabaster campus was largely empty. The town was pretty small. Maybe she'd feel Jack's presence inside a building, pulling her toward him. Or maybe he'd be looking for her.

Then she remembered he had access to the art studio. Adelaide tied EllaBella up outside Blitzer Hall and climbed the stairs.

The studio was on the top floor. It had sloping ceilings and smelled of paint and turpentine. Because it was summer, most of the easels leaned against the walls. The tables were covered with canvas tarps. Adelaide found Jack sitting there, halfway illuminated by the sunlight that streamed through the window.

"What's up." Jack said it like a statement.

"Oh, hi. I was just— I need some paint. For my Set Design project."

"In the closet."

"Sorry to interrupt."

"It's okay. Closet's right over there."

Adelaide took a jar of white paint and a jar of black, not needing either of them. She wanted to talk to him, to be witty, to get him to go somewhere with her, to make him flirt with her again. Somehow, her charm would not turn on. She couldn't always access it.

"See you around," she said. Stupidly. Ineffectually.

"Bye then," said Jack.

Adelaide found Jack sitting there, in the art studio, halfway illuminated by the sunlight that streamed through the windows.

"What's up." Jack said it like a statement.

"I came by to see you," she said. "I thought maybe you'd want to get lunch." She had already eaten two jam sandwiches, but it didn't matter.

"Can't. Sorry. I have plans."

"You do?"

"Yup." He wasn't looking at her. He was still painting, leaning forward to see exactly where his brush was touching the canvas.

"You could at least look at me," she said, feeling a rush of anger that was more at Mikey than at Jack. "You could at least see me, here, talking to you."

He looked up at her. "I just met you this morning," he said. "I don't owe you anything. I don't even remember your name."

"I came by to see you," Adelaide said. "I thought maybe you'd want to get lunch." She wasn't hungry, but it didn't matter.

"I could eat."

It wasn't an *enthusiastic* yes. Adelaide stood in the doorway, uncertain of her welcome. "There's a diner with a bacon and egg sandwich," she said. "They wrap it in foil."

Jack got off his stool and came over. His backpack was on a table by the door. "Sure, if it's wrapped in foil, I'm there."

"Or we could do the cafeteria," she said.

"No, no. Foil all the way."

She stood outside the art studio, looking through the window in the door.

Jack sat in there, half-lit by a shaft of sunlight from the

window, painting. Adelaide was filled with longing—to touch him, to take care of him, to learn his secrets. His deep brown eyes with their thick, silky lashes—she wanted them to look at her rather than at the painting. They were filled with a complexity that made her curious about him in a way she'd never been with Mikey. Mikey never seemed to have secrets, or pain; he wasn't an artist.

Well, he was a photographer, but he didn't make things from nothing, from the inside of his mysterious head. The way Jack did. The way Jack was doing right now.

His concentration was so complete, so beautiful, she couldn't interrupt it. Also, she felt shy.

Instead of talking to him, she went downstairs and walked with EllaBella down to the lake. It was nice to have the dog for company.

Two days after Adelaide met Jack, philosophers began creeping onto campus. There were signs posted on noticeboards in nearly every building hallway. They read "Welcome to the Illogic of the Multiverse, a Philosophy Intensive."

Alabaster Preparatory Academy didn't run summer programs. It rented its facilities out for groups. College students were coming for a six-week summer program about, apparently, the multiverse. The flyers announced course locations, meeting schedules, film series, and panel discussions.

The philosophers lugged duffel bags and coffeemakers. They were only nineteen or twenty years old, but they all had the serious look of people who choose to spend their summer off from college doing more college. Some faculty arrived too, professorial types with black adult suitcases on rollers, sweating in the heat as they lugged their bags upstairs.

Adelaide was buying a Diet Coke at the vending machine when a philosopher stopped to ask questions. She was a willowy young woman, maybe twenty, with brown skin and very thick dark hair that looked like it had been straightened. She was dressed all in black—a menswear jacket, black jeans, black T-shirt—with brightly colored running shoes on her feet. She asked for directions to the campus gymnasium, and then to the post office.

They got to talking. Her name was Perla Izad. She was a student at Wash U in St. Louis, studying philosophy of mind— "Perception. Mental function. Consciousness. That kind of thing." She had plantar fasciitis. She didn't have a boyfriend. Well, not anymore. Did the gymnasium have a pool? Was there a bar nearby?

Yes. And Adelaide didn't know.

How was the cafeteria food?

There was unlimited ranch dressing.

Where did Adelaide want to go to college?

Ugh. A touchy subject.

Was she interested in philosophy?

Maybe. Adelaide didn't know.

Perla explained multiverse this way: "It's a beautiful day, right?"

"Right."

"And we can agree upon this true statement: *It's not raining.* Correct?"

"Correct."

"Well. That statement implies that sometimes, in our world, it does rain. Right?"

"Uh-huh."

"And we can also say truthfully: *It isn't raining blobs of peach Jell-O today.*"

"Yup."

"Okay, then what we have implied is, *It* could have *rained blobs of peach Jell-O*, yeah? And even though there is obviously no way it rains blobs of Jell-O in *our* world, the fact that we *can say it at all* implies the existence of parallel universes where it *does* rain peach Jell-O, other possible worlds," said Perla. "There's got to be another possible world for every way that our world might have been but isn't. That's what our symposium is on. It's an idea from this guy David Lewis," she explained. "It's controversial. But whatever. Everything in philosophy is controversial."

Then she asked whether there was a sauna. And whether there was air-conditioning in the library. And did Adelaide want to go to a party? Because Perla was going to a party that night.

"What kind of party?"

"A philosophy party. Kicking off the intensive." It was at the home of Martin Schlegel, a classics teacher at Alabaster. Perla had been promised "a cheese plate of surpassing beauty" by someone who knew what was up with the catering. "I'm nervous," she said. "About the party. Is my hair all right? I hate humidity."

"Your hair is spectacular."

"It's not the kind of party where I relax and act like my real self. It's the kind of party where I watch my alcohol intake and try to talk to professors."

"That doesn't sound like a party at all."

35

"The food will be good. You should come," Perla said. "It'll be nice to have a friendly face there."

Adelaide said yes. There wasn't anything else to do, and she wanted to stop thinking about Mikey Double L.

Also, she was flattered that an actual college woman would notice her. Even someone as desperate as Perla.

They met up that evening in front of Wren Hall, Adelaide's old dormitory. Perla was holding a paper map of the campus and carrying her jacket, which was too warm for the heat of the evening.

They walked past the chapel, through an avenue of trees, and through the brick gateway that marked the edge of the *campus*. Two blocks later, they arrived at Mr. Schlegel's. Adelaide had never had him for class, since he taught Greek, but her father had become friendly with him. Maybe not actual friends, but she knew Levi had invited Schlegel and Kaspian-Lee to his home for dinner.

The downstairs of the house was jam-packed with people. They were standing on the porch, sitting on the railing and in the porch swing, leaning forward and gesticulating with their hands. They talked low and intensely, without the squeals or big laughs that Adelaide thought of as the noise of parties.

B-Cake was tied by her leash to a post. She lay sleeping on the lawn, her belly exposed.

"I know that dog," Adelaide said to Perla. She bent down and stroked B-Cake's awkward pink belly. The dog lifted her

36

head slightly. *Oh, it's you*, B-Cake said. *Yeah, I thought you might be at this party.*

They went inside. Perla disappeared immediately into the crowd. Adelaide got trapped in the foyer by Sunny Kaspian-Lee.

The teacher wore a large navy garment that was more triangular than dress-shaped, tiny white socks, and brown men's oxfords. Her black hair was cut sharp at the chin. There were lines in her forehead. She was shorter than Adelaide by several inches. "Adelaide Buchwald, you know you owe me a model." She clutched Adelaide's arm and spoke with a serious intensity.

Ugh. Of course Adelaide knew. She had the D in Global and the failing grade in Set Design.

"Come with me now," said Kaspian-Lee. "We'll discuss."

Adelaide had already met with her teachers, and for Global, there was nothing she could do. She had to take the grade. But Kaspian-Lee had given her an extension, since she'd had an A in Design for the Theater, fall term. And if Adelaide got a B or higher on the final set design project, she wouldn't be kicked out of Alabaster.

Her parents had been weirdly calm on the subject of her grades. Her father did say, in his gentle way, "Do you want to go back and live with Mom and Toby? Maybe this is your way of telling me you don't want to be at Alabaster."

But Adelaide *did* want to be at Alabaster. Mikey was there. And she loved the freedom of living in the residence halls. Also, she didn't want to go to Baltimore. It was too intense and suffocating.

Her father said softly, "You do know Alabaster's not free, right? It's reduced tuition, and they take it out of my salary."

Adelaide knew. She was ashamed. But Levi didn't yell or say how disappointed he was. He just asked if she thought she could complete the necessary work over the summer.

She told him yes.

The assignment was to plan a set for *Fool for Love* by Sam Shepard, then to build a set model for it, then defend the model verbally, to the teacher, in a project-based assessment. That is, Kaspian-Lee would quiz Adelaide about why she'd done what she'd done, and Adelaide needed to be able to explain it. Adelaide could use the studio classroom over the summer.

Now Kaspian-Lee walked Adelaide through the party to the kitchen, where the countertops were covered in wine bottles. She refilled her cup, which was made of red plastic. "Have you read the play?"

"Of course." Adelaide had only read the first five pages. She knew it took place in a motel room.

"You have to get on it," said Kaspian-Lee. "I say this with respect. Why would you fail my class? You are very capable."

"Thank you."

"You measure correctly. Almost nobody measures correctly. And your glue is neat. I say this to encourage you. You simply have to stop mooning and force yourself to do this project."

"I know. I'm sorry."

"This is my lover's house," said Kaspian-Lee, opening the freezer. "I am entitled to go in here. I'm not being rude." She took out some ice. "Let's get cheese before it's gone. Look, people have decimated the Brie. They don't know how to cut it properly, these philosophers."

"How are you supposed to cut it?"

"It should always form a triangle. You don't chop off the

point. Here, eat this, it's a Morbier. Have you had a Morbier? It's one of the best-looking cheeses. And look, fig jam. The philosophers have ruined that, too."

Adelaide ate the Morbier and Kaspian-Lee turned abruptly to a tall, heavy young man, only about seventeen, wearing a blue button-down with the sleeves rolled up. "Will you play now?" she asked him.

The young man shrugged. "If you want."

"I do want," she said. "Adelaide, this is Oscar. He's here to play the piano."

"Hi, Adelaide."

"Hi, Oscar."

Oscar took a suit jacket off the piano bench and put it on, despite the heat. He sat down and began to play.

Adelaide had never thought about the piano in her life. She had never listened to classical music. But Oscar rained on the keys with an enormous concentration. She did admire it.

Kaspian-Lee disappeared. The philosophers swarmed, anxious and argumentative, talking as if conversation were blood sport.

Adelaide was suddenly very hungry. She grabbed the misshapen Brie by its rind and huddled with it in a corner, where she leaned against a bookshelf and watched the party. She ate the cheese like a slice of pizza and thought,

Toby is an addict. Toby is an addict.

Her brain settled into the thought. It was an old habit, whenever she had a moment, undistracted.

Of course, Adelaide's mother and father always said Toby was *sick*. Or *ill*.

Sick and *ill* are what the medical establishment suggests you say. The words are accurate, but to be clear, Toby went to rehab at age fourteen.

Fourteen.

At one point, he needed to get high so badly that in order to get a prescription, he smashed his own wrist with a hammer.

Then, when the scrip ran out, he told them

he was sick with migraines. He told them

his wrist still hurt. He got another jar of pills, and another.

When he couldn't fake pain, he stole Adelaide's money. And their parents' money. He told them

he was sleeping over at Ian's house. He told them

he was exhausted from basketball practice, so exhausted he couldn't keep his head up, when in truth, he was nodding off.

He told them

he was throwing up because of stomach pain when really, the nausea was a side effect of narcotics; he told them

he had a virus. He went back to

saying he had migraines.

He was taken to a neurologist, and a headache expert.

He frightened his parents. They thought he might have a brain tumor.

When Toby went to rehab, his addiction taxed the family's financial resources sorely. The Buchwalds sold their home and the Good Sheep Yarn Shop, spent their savings, and then spent Levi's pension money. While they knew they were lucky as hell to have the funds at all, they were looking at a very different future than the one they had saved for.

The thing that bothered Adelaide most was the loss of Toby himself. He had disappeared on her, even when they were in the same room.

She knew she was supposed to hold him blameless. She knew he had susceptible brain chemistry. There was an opioid epidemic across the nation. It was a social problem. A structural problem.

Levi tried to stay balanced, burying himself in a book he was writing about teaching Shakespeare in the high school classroom, emerging to be warmly present and loving for about a half hour in the morning and an hour at night. He would be chatty and upbeat, focused completely on sharing bits about his day, listening to Adelaide and Rebecca. He made garlicky pasta and did the dishes before declaring himself tuckered out and going to bed. It seemed to Adelaide that Levi was giving all that he could. If they asked him for any more, he might collapse.

Rebecca tried to match Levi's attempts at normalcy and connection, but she flailed wildly from self-hatred (blaming her own parenting for Toby's addiction) to fury at the factors other than herself that had led to it. Had she been too permissive, or too strict? she'd wonder aloud. Had she been too smothering, or too involved with her career? How could those idiot other parents leave addictive drugs in their medicine cabinets for anyone to find? How irresponsible were they, leaving their teenagers home alone to throw wild parties? And the problem with opioids wasn't simply caused by overprescription, like so many people thought. Rebecca researched the epidemic in her spare time and told Adelaide all about her reading. The drug crisis was caused by social and economic upheaval. Even though middle-class kids like Toby were the ones the media often wrote about, most addicts were people struggling with poverty, trauma, and ill health. Rebecca investigated wide-ranging solutions like harm-reduction services, faith-based healing, government regulation, and lowered barriers to care. Mostly, in the day-to-day, she managed Toby's health: insurance claims, therapists, doctors, researching factors that led to successful recovery. It wasn't long before Rebecca became nearly overcome with pain from sciatica.

Post-therapy, the Buchwalds told Adelaide it was

normal for her to feel anger. They also told her she should let go of that

normal anger, even though it was

normal anger, and remind herself that

Toby got sick.

It was the illness that did everything, they said.

The illness, not him.

Addiction changes the way the brain functions on a molecular level. That's why it's a disease. The shift in brain chemistry made it impossible for Toby to stop without help.

Adelaide answered *Yes, yes, of course.* She wanted to be compassionate. But she couldn't help but feel that Toby cared more about

getting a fix,

than he did about her,

than he did about their parents.

He had left her. His wheezing sounded in her dreams each night to remind Adelaide how close he'd come to dying, and how little he seemed to care that it hurt her.

Toby is an addict.

✛ ✛ ✛

Now, at the philosophy party, a second refrain: *Mikey doesn't love me. Mikey doesn't love me.*

Adelaide wondered: If she weren't sad underneath her charm and painted nails, would Mikey have loved her all the way?

If she weren't so talky, would he?

If she were wickedly funny, if she were mysterious and reserved instead of sparkly, if she were thinner or taller?

If she were a girl with more dramatically viable eyebrows, Adelaide felt, Mikey would never have left her. Or if she were a girl with long coltish legs and the kind of figure that draped over furniture.

She thought these things over and over, like a compulsion, even though she knew she should know better.

The cheese grew squashy in her hand. She bit off a big chunk and tongued it. She felt something of the thrill she remembered from stealing cookies from the cooling rack when her mother baked for holiday parties.

Then Jack appeared.

He was in the far left portion of her vision, talking to an elderly philosopher and wearing jeans and a gray T-shirt. His gold skin glowed.

Adelaide turned her head to look. Jack's grin spread across his face. He reached up slowly to wipe the sweat off the back of his neck.

He was

exquisite.

He turned and saw Adelaide staring.

He said something to the elderly philosopher and came over to her.

He leaned down. She felt his lips against her ear. "Will you hide me?" he asked.

"Yes," she answered.

"Now?"

She nodded. "Follow me."

Aware of her hair against her forehead and the pumping of blood in her temples, Adelaide led Jack through the kitchen and out the back door.

They stepped into the thick summer air of Martin Schlegel's yard. It was covered in summer roses and crawling vines. There was a smell of green. At the back of the yard was a white rope hammock strung between two trees. The sound of Oscar's piano playing trickled out.

They sat awkwardly on the edge of the hammock, their feet still on the grass.

"What are you hiding from?" Adelaide asked.

"It all."

"The party?"

"Myself at the party."

"How so?"

"I was lying to that philosopher."

———————————

He turned and saw Adelaide staring.

He said something to the elderly philosopher and came over to her.

He leaned down. She felt his lips against her ear. "Will you hide me?"

She grabbed his arm and pulled him into Schlegel's half-bathroom. It was lit by a single tangerine-scented candle. It had illusion prints on the wall. A small row of cardboard 3-D glasses hung from hooks next to the towel rack.

Jack closed the door gently, a finger to his lips.

"Why are you hiding?" Adelaide asked.

"There's a girl here I used to know. From back when."

"When what?"

"It's embarrassing."

"Tell me."

He sighed. "Before we moved to Spain, I went to Alabaster, right? I was in ninth and she was a senior. She must be in college now. And she's here."

"What's the problem?"

"I made a fool of myself."

"How?"

"Poetry. I wrote her, like, a poem a day. I think I kind of stalked her, but I imagined I was dashing and romantic. I imagined her smiling as she found another envelope, reading my words over and over. But she was just trashing them and finally she told me to stop." Jack laughed and shook his head. "I'm appalled that I ever did that." He was leaning against the sink.

Adelaide reached for a pair of 3-D glasses. "Put these on so we can see the art properly."

He put his on as she took a second pair. "Oh my."

"What?"

"Here, you need to . . . Wait, shut your eyes." He adjusted her glasses. "Now turn. Now open."

"Oh what? Are they . . ."

"Yes, they absolutely are." Jack collapsed, laughing. "Schlegel is a filthy-minded man."

"Can you hide me?"

"Why?" she asked.

His hair curled in the heat. "I need to get away from B-Cake."

"I saw her outside."

"She's inside now, and she's been sitting in my lap for the past fifteen minutes. I'm covered in dog fur."

"I can't hide you from B-Cake. She locates things by smell."

"Do I smell?"

It was the sort of thing Adelaide would never ask someone. She would worry that she did in fact smell, and smelled bad in some way, like sweat or nerves. Or like soup. You know, the way some people smell like soup.

She leaned in and smelled Jack's neck.

He smelled faintly of coconut shampoo. Or maybe it was sunblock. She wanted to put her lips on the soft part of his ear.

Someone knocked on the door of the bathroom.

"Not now!" Jack called, laughing.

"Shhh!"

"Oh right, we're hiding."

"When two of us leave," said Adelaide, "they're going to think we were hooking up in here."

"No. We're innocently talking about 3-D pornography," said Jack.

"But we'll come out of the bathroom together."

Jack started laughing again, not a disengaged, ironic laugh, like so many boys at Alabaster cultivated, but a slightly manic, hysterical laugh, like he might be panicking, or enjoying himself very much indeed.

"Why didn't you just leave the party?" Adelaide asked. "When you saw the poetry woman."

"I saw you eating Brie in the corner."

She kissed him then. She reached up and ran her finger along the soft fuzz at the back of his neck. Their mouths joined incredibly lightly, so lightly she could hardly be sure their lips had touched.

Then she was sure.

"I like the way you laugh," she said, when they separated for a moment. He kissed her again and she loved him, she really did. In the kiss it seemed like they had known one another for centuries. He touched her collarbone with his warm fingers. Her blood rushed to her head, and she could feel it pounding through her.

As she leaned back against the bookshelf after smelling Jack's neck, Adelaide thought:

I could go home with him tonight.

47

I could go home with him
the same week Mikey left me.
I could do that.
I could make Mikey feel terrible,
if Mikey ever knew.

Adelaide put her hand gently on Jack's arm. "You smell good to me."

Jack smiled and shook his head a little. "I've had too much of an unfamiliar drink," he said. He pulled away and hitched his jeans up. "I should get myself home. Good night, and good luck to you."

"Great," she said. "Fine. Good night and good luck."

Adelaide ate her triangle of Brie quietly in the corner, listening to Oscar the piano player.

The music was turbulent. It made her feel as if the sky was about to break open, and as if

Mikey not loving her and

Toby being an addict

were being pushed through the music

into the sky. Somehow, this pianist

knew how she felt,

knew the storm that was in her, a storm of self-pity and sadness and anger and fatigue at being

sparkly, at keeping people

happy.

The philosophers gathered round the piano, their conversation hushed.

B-Cake flopped on the rug with her belly up.

Oscar finished playing. He stood and blended into the crowd.

Someone switched on a playlist and turned up the volume on the speakers. The college-age philosophers began dancing in Schlegel's living room, pressing in from the kitchen and porch. They danced in a stiff-armed way, tossing back their heads and singing the lyrics.

"What lie did you tell the philosopher?" Adelaide asked.

"I said I'd read Jürgen Habermas," said Jack, "because he asked me, 'Have you read Jürgen Habermas?' And I said 'A little,' when the answer is 'Not at all.' And then he said—"

Here, Jack lay back onto the width of the hammock, with his feet still on the ground. Adelaide's eyes went to his abdomen before she forced them back to his face.

"He said incomprehensible things about Jürgen Habermas, and I said, 'Right you are.' And he said more incomprehensible things and I said, 'I never thought of it that way.' Truth is, I hated myself for not understanding. And I hated myself for pretending to understand rather than asking him to explain. And I also hated myself for not wanting to understand about Jürgen Habermas, really, at all, because you know. School. You're supposed to want to know Jürgen Habermas."

"Jürgen Habermas is a funny name," Adelaide said. She had never heard of Habermas at all. "If you just say it over and over."

"Jürgen."

"Jürgen."

"We shouldn't make fun of someone's name," Jack said.

"You're right," she said.

"You're very pretty, Adelaide."

She lay back slowly in the hammock so she was next to him.

Jack grabbed her hand and they burst out of the bathroom, laughing, running out of Schlegel's house and around the corner. They collapsed against a mailbox, laughing. "Did anyone see us?" Jack asked.

"I think we were invisible."

They walked together through the darkened campus, past the avenue of trees and the huge dome of the library to the sciences building, Millhauser Hall. Adelaide knew how to get up on the roof. You climbed out a window and then up a fire escape.

"I was fourteen last time I was on this campus," said Jack, when they'd reached the roof. "It's so weird to be back."

"What kind of school did you go to in Spain?"

"An American school. In Barcelona."

"Did you study in English?"

He nodded. "The kids were American or English, mostly, but some were from other parts of the world. Fifty-five nations, they were always saying. And we all took Spanish." Jack was leaning against the wall at the edge of the roof, and Adelaide was standing two feet away. "Come here," he said.

"Why?" She knew why.

"Just come here. If you want to."

She stepped up and he took both sides of her face in his hands and kissed her like it mattered to him, holding her face like it was a precious thing, rubbing his thumb gently across her cheekbone and then her jaw.

Mikey had never kissed her like that. Never like
it mattered so much. Never
so tenderly.
All that time with Mikey Double L, he'd kissed her like
it was fun, like
it was a game, like
he was turned on, but
not like he
cherished her.
Never.

She pulled away and covered her face with her hands.

"What's wrong?" Jack asked.

"Nothing."

"Something's wrong. I didn't mean to—"

"You didn't. It's not that. I'm fine, really."

"I'm sorry. I thought—"

"I came over when you asked me to. I wanted to. Don't worry. You probably think I've had a trauma or abuse or something, but I haven't," she blurted. "I'm just a mess for other reasons." She swallowed. "I should go home now."

"Of course. Of course. I'll walk you back."

They climbed down the fire escape.

While they walked, Adelaide wept silently. She felt overwhelmingly stupid. She had ruined everything with
her unsavory, unwanted

sadness, sadness that made her

unlovable and burdensome, sadness that was

maybe anger in disguise,

maybe anger, leaking out of her,

because there was nobody to yell at,

nobody to vent it on,

no way to burn it off. It had to come out.

She didn't know if she was angry at

Mikey or at

Toby. And she didn't know if her anger had ruined things with

Mikey or

Toby, or now with

Jack—

or all three.

She said goodbye quickly, ran up to her bedroom in her dad's office space, and crawled into the foldout, still wearing her clothes. She turned out her light—and then remembered the dogs.

She hadn't walked them.

She hauled herself up again and put on a sweater. Found her shoes. She walked each dog separately (except the two who lived together), going to one house and then another, in the ugly, shuddering chill of the night.

4

ADELAIDE'S BROTHER

Toby and Adelaide. Ages nine and eleven.

TOBY: (snorts up snot in a gross way)

ADELAIDE: Oh no, you don't. Stop that.

TOBY: I'm just sniffing. (snorts up snot)

ADELAIDE: Nuh-uh. It's too disgusting.

TOBY: I can't help it. (snorts up snot)

ADELAIDE: Get a tissue. Here. Here's a tissue.

TOBY: (blows very weakly into the tissue) Nothing
comes out.

ADELAIDE: Blow it hard, silly.

TOBY: (snorts up snot)

ADELAIDE: I'm going to punish you when you do that.

TOBY: You can't punish me. Only Mom and Dad can
punish me.

ADELAIDE: I can figure out a way.

TOBY: How?

ADELAIDE: By saying swear words.

TOBY: I hate swear words!

ADELAIDE: I know you do. I think if I swear whenever
you snort up your snot, then you'll stop doing it.

TOBY: (snorts up snot)

ADELAIDE: Poop!

TOBY: (snorts up snot)

ADELAIDE: Weiner!

TOBY: (snorts up snot)

ADELAIDE: Thunder-butt!

TOBY: What?

ADELAIDE: Thunder-butt. Whenever you snort your
snot, I'm going to say "poop weiner thunder-butt."

TOBY: You will?

ADELAIDE: I'll say it in front of your friends. And your
teachers. You'll do a snort and I'll be all, *Poop
weiner thunder-butt*. Super loud. Everyone will
be shocked. You'll be too embarrassed to snort
anymore.

TOBY: Say it again!

ADELAIDE: No.

TOBY: Say it again!

ADELAIDE: You like it now? *You* say it.

TOBY: No. I'm not saying swears.

✛ ✛ ✛

Adelaide remembered picking Toby up from a weekend Dungeons and Dragons game at Boston Strategy Lab, a board-game club he belonged to. She was twelve and he was ten. "How was your campaign?"

"Good. But I lost an arm."

"What?"

"It's no biggie. My evil twin turned into a werewolf and bit it off."

"Was it your fighting arm?"

"Yeah," said Toby cheerfully. "But I can regrow it. Or get a wooden one or something. Plus I turned into a werewolf right back and I bit off his leg. Stuff like that happens all the time. Can we get M&M's?"

She took him into a drugstore and bought M&M's for both of them. "D and D and M and M," he said as they walked the rest of the way home. He liked to eat the green ones and make wishes. He consumed all the green ones back to back, doing wishes in a row. Then he opened his mouth with crushed-up green M&M's in it.

She gave him licks of her ice cream cones. She made him toast. She read to him. She gave him her time, playing Unstable Unicorns and Exploding Kittens. Their relationship had always been characterized by Adelaide giving and Toby taking, but she'd been delighted, most of the time, to play protector or indulgent older sibling.

In return, he made her laugh. And if he got too greedy, she just batted his hand and told him he couldn't have whatever it was he wanted.

Adelaide was proud of Toby. He was popular in middle

school, a short boy even the tall girls liked. People would say, "Are you Toby Buchwald's sister? He's so cute." Eighth-grade girls, when he was only in seventh. And Adelaide was glad to answer yes.

When he got to high school—it was public school in Boston then—he had a similar effect on women. He had shaggy dark hair and a mouth full of braces. He talked to everyone. He was a puppy of a boy, clowning and bright. His smart mouth and swagger made up for what he lacked in height, and rather than go out with a ninth grader, he became the much-adored pet of a group of popular seniors. They started by offering him rides home. Then they'd bring him with them after school when they went to get smoothies. Pretty soon he sat with them at lunch. They picked him up in their cars and took him with them, wherever they were going.

Adelaide wasn't paying attention. She was sleeping over at Ashlee's and doing track and field. She started going to art museums with Veronica sometimes. Also she went out with this guy Mateo for a little and then with William for a little, and though neither was serious, they took up time. She baby-sat quite a lot. And sometimes there were parties. She was, in essence, a fairly centered, fairly happy person, without the flash and sparkle she prided herself on now, without the talky edge she'd developed. She was milder then. Less in need of distraction.

Adelaide didn't know how Toby made that decision, first to take something out of a medicine cabinet. She never would have. For her, it wasn't very hard to say

"Nah, that's stupid risky," or

"Not for me today," or even

"Don't pressure me. It's so gross."

She'd said those things at parties, or with friends. Plenty of times. Why couldn't Toby?

What she did know was, the pills became routine for him. Every weekend. Some weeknights. Other kids were doing it too. One dad had a supply of oxycodone he had never thrown out. A mom had a pill habit. And so on. Toby's perennial grin hid a stripe of anxiety and depression, and the pills alleviated it.

One night he found a full jar of Percocet in some parent's bathroom. He stole it, and took some every day. And once it was a habit, his body demanded it. Without cease.

When the bottle ran out, that's when Toby broke his own wrist. He

iced it first, took two Advil, and

whacked his left wrist

repeatedly

with the hammer held in his right.

He took himself to the hospital before calling anyone, having planned it out ahead of time, the bus route and everything. He told the doctors he'd dropped a twenty-pound weight while working out. He rated his pain a ten on a scale of one to ten and ended up with an Oxy prescription, legit as legit could be.

But the prescription ran out soon enough. So he started buying.

Sure, Adelaide ran into Toby at parties sometimes, though she wasn't friends with his crowd. When she did, she thought he was drunk. A lightweight. He'd tell her he had two beers.

It didn't seem horrible for a fourteen-year-old to have two beers. Adelaide's parents didn't forbid her to drink. They lectured her: a glass of water for every serving of booze; stay away from the hard stuff and stick to wine or beer. Eat if you're having alcohol so it doesn't hit your system too hard. Never get in a car driven by someone who's been drinking. Don't make out with people if you're drunk, since you might have trouble saying what you want and don't want. Or the other person might not hear it clearly. Don't take drinks from strangers: pour or open your own. They had told her all this, and offered to pick her up anywhere, any time she needed a ride home.

They had trusted her judgment. And Toby's.

When Toby finally went to the hospital and then to rehab, Adelaide put it all together. She realized why Toby had fallen asleep on her so

limply and childishly, that time they'd taken the bus home from that party.

She realized he wasn't always at Ian's and why

he was broke despite his allowance.

Her parents coped. Levi immersed himself in health insurance and treatment options. Rebecca handled all Toby's appointments, talked to all the doctors, and spoke to Toby himself. Adelaide talked to Toby's teachers and called his friends' parents, explaining what had happened; what might be happening with *their* kids.

She was glad to have something to do. It was good to be busy, rather than spend her time thinking about

Toby shooting up, about

Toby wasting away, about

Toby's mind, and whether somewhere in there, he might still be the brother she loved, now that his brain chemistry was permanently altered.

Rebecca was especially grateful for Adelaide's assistance. She wrapped her daughter in big, squashy hugs, the kind Adelaide had loved as a child. Rebecca was curvy, with long curly hair that echoed the texture of the dense sweaters she made and wore. Even on hot days, dressed in a T-shirt and wide-leg pants, she seemed faintly wooly. She told Adelaide she was the best possible help; Adelaide was so mature, was keeping them all together, thank you thank you.

The family had been led to believe it would just be ninety days in Kingsmont, the rehab center, but Toby began having episodes. Rebecca said Toby would rage and scream. Maybe the drugs had done something to his brain. He'd be better soon, hopefully. He was going on medication.

That was when Adelaide and Levi moved to Baltimore to be with Rebecca.

The new school was okay. It was hard to make friends at first. There was a script in Adelaide's head.

My little brother is in rehab.

My little brother is in rehab.

Everywhere she went, a rhythm beat beneath her feet.

Toby is an addict.

Toby is an addict.

Those words were scrawled across her face for everyone to see. They were written on her ankles and her hands, every visible part of her. People would ask how she was. Adelaide would say, "Fine." She'd say, "Great." She'd say what they wanted to hear.

But what she answered in her head was *My little brother is in rehab.*

At first, she went along on the Kingsmont weekly visiting day. But Toby wouldn't look at her. He didn't speak to her. And she could barely speak to him.

She was humiliated to find that she always cried, from the minute her mother parked the car. Not loud crying. Silent. Just her eyes pouring water and her throat closed. She couldn't stop it. She cried because Toby's face looked different. The way he held his arms at his sides was peculiar. She cried because she didn't know him anymore, couldn't see her little brother inside this stranger.

Nobody taught him how to shave, and he needed to now. He had a wispy mustache. His teeth didn't look clean. There were no books by his bedside. No games in his room.

Soon her parents gently suggested Adelaide not come along. They said they didn't want Toby to see her cry like that. "Addicts often feel judged by their family and friends," said the therapist at one visit, when Toby wasn't in the room. "You should refrain from negativity as much as possible."

The Buchwalds worried her crying would make Toby anxious and guilty. He already knew the effects his actions had had on the family. Now he was building a new sense of himself as a sober person.

Also, they hated seeing her cry. It exhausted them, taking care of Adelaide on top of taking care of Toby.

They didn't say that. But Adelaide could tell: they needed her to be strong.

Rebecca said, "Don't force yourself, pudding. You have done so much for the family already. We haven't forgotten. It's okay to sit this one out."

Levi said, "It might be easier on Toby if it's just the two of us, this visit. And that's okay. He won't ever forget how much you love him."

She stopped visiting. It was something of a relief. Instead, she began writing Toby letters. Paper letters.

Hi, Toby.

Here's the home update. Full of thrills!

Dad made a grain bowl involving bok choy, mushrooms, and ground chicken. He is calling it dinner, but I am not certain it can legally be called that.

Mom and her sciatica, OMG. She will not do her exercises. She sets the mat out. And it's right in the middle of the living room. She moves the coffee table to one side, gets it all set up. And then it sits there all day Saturday. Reproaching her.

The exercises literally take her seven minutes, but she doesn't do them and then her ass hurts and she's sad.

She took me shopping for rain boots and I was like,

"These ones, please." And she said,

"Maybe you want some different ones; do you want to try on some more?" And I was like,

"No thank you, I like these. They have red polka-dots. Red polka-dots are my dream." And she was like,

"Maybe you should try on the green." And I was like,

"It's the same boot, just a different color." And she was like,

"Maybe you want to try on those flowered ones, then?" And I was like,

"I'm super into these red polka-dots, thank you very much."

But whatever, we got through it and now I have rain boots.

I hit the Museum of Visionary Art today with Ling. Things we saw include:

the world's first robot family and

a series of automatons, like mechanical people.

Also a kid with literally so much snot it hung in a ribbon from her nose.

Then we got Dippin' Dots.

Poop weiner thunder-butt
and lots of love, Adelaide.

He didn't answer.

Not once. Not ever never. So Adelaide tried harder. She bought

postcards of Marimekko prints and DC Comics heroes and wrote cheery notes, talking about celebrity gossip, reporting on school dances and interesting project and clubs.

She performed

forgiveness and kindness, over and over.

She never showed any

anger or disappointment.

In fact, it was in these letters that the first version of Adelaide's sparkly, talky persona began to emerge. She wanted to entertain Toby. To get a response from him. And she found that in assuming the sparkle, putting it on like a sequined jacket, she could alleviate a little of her distress.

Adelaide waited for a letter in return. Or just a note.

What was he doing with his time at Kingsmont, anyway? There were free periods. He could write if he wanted to.

Toby remained at the Kingsmont Center until May, when he moved to Future House, a sober-living boarding home for high schoolers. Living there, he went to summer classes at a clean-and-sober high school. He did okay. Their parents visited him every weekend, just as before.

Eventually, Adelaide stopped writing. She spent the summer before heading to Alabaster working in a doggie day care with her friend Ling, who had a cousin who knew a guy who owned it. After work, they'd meet up at Joelle's, sit on her back porch, drink beer they got with Joelle's fake ID, and order pizza.

There were some boys they liked, who maybe liked them back.

Sometimes the boys would come over.

Sometimes there was a party somewhere.

If there was nothing else to do, Adelaide, Ling, and Joelle would go get spicy noodles and window-shop.

But still,

even with Toby all right,

or kind of all right,

or all right for the time being,

Adelaide slept badly and thought obsessively. She would think,

What if he relapses?

What if he dies?

What am I doing on this porch, eating pizza as the sun sets, when my parents have spent half their retirement savings to pay for Toby's treatment?

What am I doing kissing this boy, when Toby is still this gray lump of a person, weighed down by shame and medication, staring blankly at the wall every evening?

How can I drink this beer when people become alcoholics? This is a dangerous substance, and maybe some

demon of addiction is

lurking inside me,

sucking up this alcohol, and

one day I'll wake up and feel like I need it more than anything.

But she still drank the beer. And ate the pizza. And kissed the boy, though it wasn't serious.

She was leaving town in late August. Her friends would all spend junior year in Baltimore, and she would go with her father up to Alabaster.

She felt nostalgic for the very summer she was living, for those evenings at Joelle's, for the aching way the boy made her feel when he kissed her, even though he was a little vacant and he didn't make her laugh. She had never before thought of her own life with nostalgia as she'd lived it—but that summer it was overwhelming.

This will never happen again, she thought.

We will never be like this again.

Hold on to this feeling.

Remember it.

And yet, she also experienced waves of disassociation from it all. It wouldn't last, so why did it matter? Come fall, she'd be in northern Massachusetts. Come fall, she'd have different friends. Who cared what happened with any of it?

She brought Toby's Lego bin up from the basement. He used to build kits, back in elementary school. Star Wars, Harry Potter, rescue vehicles. Adelaide would sit by him sometimes and assist. He could follow the most complicated instructions, but he liked his sister to find the pieces he needed. He'd empty the plastic bags into cereal bowls, sometimes having as many as ten bowls around him on their family room floor.

Now pieces of those kits were mixed together in an enormous clear plastic box along with random tiny community workers in Lego uniforms, fake flowerpots, and regular Lego bricks. Adelaide began making dioramas.

Joelle's deck with the hot tub.

Ling's car, parked outside her house.

The doggie day care.

Making the dioramas used up some of the
churning energy Adelaide had inside, the
nostalgia mixed with
sadness over Toby, the
almost-unbearable poignancy of it all.

5

THE PRECARIOUS
NATURE OF NEW LOVE

The morning after Mr. Schlegel's philosophy party, Adelaide woke up thinking of Jack. How he smelled, how his neck had felt under her fingertips, how curious she was to see his heart. She liked the soft way he pronounced some of his *L*s, maybe a leftover from his time in Spain, and the way he ran his fingers through his hair absentmindedly, usually making it look worse.

Maybe he would be at the dog run with B-Cake.

Maybe he would call or text.

At the dog run, EllaBella trotted around, sniffing every corner.

Lord Voldemort tried to kill a squirrel but failed.

Adelaide thought about texting Jack. But no.

She was too ashamed of crying when they'd kissed.

Adelaide texted Jack.

She felt she was in love with him. Was that impossible?
She was a rational person. Usually, anyhow.

> Thanks for walking me home.

Are you okay?

> I'm okay.

> But you know what would be good?

What?

> If you could just erase the crying bit of the evening from your memory. Erase! Please remember only up to the time when we talked about Barcelona. That would be good, if you don't mind.

Adelaide texted Jack.

She felt like she might love him. Was that impossible?
She was a rational person. Usually, anyhow.

> Thanks for walking me home.

Of course.

I'm at the dog run.

. . .

. . .

You around later?

. . .

. . .

OK. I get it.

Sorry. I just—

I have someone.

I said, I get it.

———————————————

Adelaide thought about texting Jack. She wanted to see him, but also, she was too ashamed of crying when they'd kissed.

As she was returning EllaBella to Mr. Byrd's house, though, a text from him came in.

Feel like swimming?

                              When?

Today. Dodson's Hole, at
noon. I'm going with some
guys from my job.

                              Only guys?

Not if you come with.

                              I'm supposed to work on my
                              Set Design model.

Please come.

                              I don't think I can.

                              I just broke up with someone.
                              I am an egg yolk of misery.

Come anyway.

                              He and I might get back
                              together, is all. Maybe.

What is an egg yolk of
misery?

. . .

. . .

Okay, I get it.

Sorry.

It's fine.

As she was returning EllaBella to Mr. Byrd's house, though, a text from him came in.

Feel like swimming?

When?

Today. Dodson's Hole, at
noon. I'm going with some
guys from my job.

Only guys?

Not if you come with.

Dodson's Hole was a swimming place in a state park, about forty-five minutes away. You hiked in a ways and then came across a section of lazy river with stone steps going down to it.

Someone had looped a length of rope over a thick tree that arched over the river. You could run off the dock, holding the rope, swing out, and drop in.

People laid picnic blankets and towels on a stretch of flat, sunny lawn but stayed mostly in the shade of the trees that lined the river, which created dappled green patterns on the water. Adelaide had been there on a school outing, a start-of junior year bonding thing in September.

I'm supposed to work on this
Set Design model I have to
build.

Please come.

Please.

OK.

"You can go first."

"No, you go. It's too cold."

"I'm going to rush it."

"You go ahead and rush it."

Jack was unselfconscious in a bathing suit, despite the sizable scar on his side, and his unusual leg. The leg was thin and didn't seem to have much strength. The rest of him was all shoulders and a ripple of muscle across his abdomen.

"Where are the guys from your job?" she asked him.

"Late, I guess."

They had driven to the park in Jack's car, then lugged towels and bottles of soda from the parking lot to Dodson's Hole. Adelaide wore a bikini with fern fronds on it and a pair of bright blue swimming goggles.

"Are they coming at all?"

"Yes."

He took a deep breath and rushed off the dock, swinging out and dropping into the river.

Adelaide did the same, and the chill of the water after the heat of the day made her feel wildly awake.

Later, his friends showed. One of them was Oscar, the piano player from Schlegel's party. He looked pale and slightly awkward in board shorts and a T-shirt. The other was Terrance, a slim black guy with a triangular face who hid his eyes behind dark glasses. Both of them went to the local public school and knew each other from the school orchestra. Terrance played what he called "bad oboe." They both had summer jobs with Jack at Uncle Benny's Fine Sandwiches.

The boys were comically underprepared for a day at the water. Oscar had no towel. Terrance had forgotten swimwear and just rolled up his jeans to go swimming. They had failed to bring snacks. They both got thirsty and complained about not having anything to drink. Adelaide shared her potato chips and let them finish her seltzer.

It was nice to be surrounded by boys. They showed off, cannonballing off the dock. Oscar talked about wanting to make a silent disco, with everyone on headphones. Different people would be listening to different songs, but everyone would dance together. "You'd find the person who had your same song," he said. "You could tell it was the same by the rhythm of how they danced. And the style."

"*You* could tell," said Terrance. "Everyone else would be like, walking around confused and unhappy."

"They wouldn't be unhappy," said Oscar. "They'd be dancing."

"What's the point of the disco being silent?" said Jack.

"I don't know," said Oscar. "It would just be like, a happening. Funny and kind of magical."

"Or embarrassing," said Jack.

"It would take way too much organizing," said Terrance. "Headphones for everyone and all that."

"I bet we could get funding at school," said Oscar. "Like if it was a school dance."

"Would you curate all the playlists?" asked Adelaide. "How many would there be?"

"If people have matching playlists, they're going to get ornery," said Terrance. "No one wants to dance with the one same person all night."

"I think people would start trying to choose their own music," said Adelaide. "People would off-road and change to their own songs."

"God, you're all squashing my dream," said Oscar. "Why are you squashing?"

"I'm being practical," said Terrance.

"I wasn't going to actually do it," said Oscar.

Jack touched Adelaide's back, very softly. "You want to swim? Get away from these jokers?"

"I heard that," said Terrance. "I'm swimming too."

"We're all swimming," said Oscar, standing up. "You can't escape us, Adelaide."

On the way back, with mud and shreds of grass clinging to their feet, Adelaide and Jack stopped for tacos. They ate at a food truck in a parking lot, sitting perched on a cement barrier behind a couple of orange traffic cones.

Her phone pinged. It was Mikey.

> Hey, I'm thinking of you.
> You all right?

Adelaide deleted the text and turned her phone off. "Sorry 'bout that."

"Who was it?" Jack asked.

"Nobody important."

On the way back, with mud and shreds of grass clinging to their feet, Adelaide and Jack stopped for tacos. They ate at a food truck in a parking lot, sitting perched on a cement barrier behind a couple of orange traffic cones.

Her phone pinged. It was Mikey.

> Hey, I'm thinking of you.
> You all right?

"Sorry," she told Jack. "I have to take this."

She had never not answered a text from Mikey. She couldn't ignore him now. They hadn't spoken since their breakup.

She called him, walking over to the other side of the parking lot. "Hey."

"Hey," said Mikey Double L.

"Where are you?"

"Airport. On the way to Puerto Rico."

"Wow."

"I might be nervous."

Mikey always got anxious around travel. He hated packing, worried buses would be late, planes delayed.

"You'll be okay," said Adelaide. "You got this." She kept her voice bright, as if they were old friends and she was eager to hear about his adventures.

"I already know I forgot toothpaste."

"Someone in the program will share with you."

"My Spanish should be better."

"Tell me about the trip."

Mikey talked on about his service trip, the hurricane relief work they'd be doing, where he'd be traveling. "How are the dogs you're walking?"

"Fantastic."

"That's good."

"Yeah."

"Well."

"What?"

"I just wanted to make sure you're okay," said Mikey.

"I'm super happy," said Adelaide. "Don't worry about me. Do great things in Puerto Rico."

She hung up and felt her face crumple. It was horrid talking to Mikey in this fake bright way, having him

flying across the sea, having

nothing really to say to him after wanting to talk to him constantly for so long.

It seemed impossible that so recently the two of them had been rolling around in his bed, hitting each other with pillows.

She and Jack didn't speak at all the rest of the drive home.

Adelaide looked out the window and thought

of Mikey, looking up at her when he lifted his mask after a fencing match,

of Mikey, drinking hot chocolate in the dormitory common room,

of Mikey, riding a bicycle with the yellow ribbon on the handle, grinning widely.

"We're here," said Jack, his voice cold.

Adelaide got out of the car. "Thanks for the good outing," she said.

"Sure."

He drove off without another word.

6

MIKEY DOUBLE L, A LOVE STORY IN ONLY ONE UNIVERSE

Mikey Lewis Lieu, also known as Mikey Double L, was Adelaide's first love.

He was a fencer and an optimist. He believed in positive thinking, in psyching himself up for a bout. He was dependable. He had wonderful arm muscles.

When she and Mikey started going out, November of junior year, Adelaide very quickly came to require Mikey Double L. He had such a reassuring round face, like a dinner plate, warm from washing.

Mikey Double L thought of things like

giving a girl a bicycle.

He did that. He gave Adelaide a bicycle with a yellow bow tied on one handle.

He thought of things like

texting a girl in the early morning. "Hello, sunshine."

He reached out to hold her hand as the two of them walked through campus.

A boy like that would make most anyone happy.

Adelaide wasn't depressed. She never felt bleak. She had energy. She was talky. She painted her fingernails green and wore floral-print dresses and enormous cardigan sweaters.

But you can be talky and paint your fingernails and still be very sad.

In fact, you can be talky and paint your fingernails to protect other people from how sad you are.

Adelaide couldn't find a source of happiness in herself. It just didn't seem to be there.

She could distract herself from sadness, though. For example, she built dioramas from a mix of cardboard, paint, and Lego, then filled them with Lego people and left them in the dormitory bathroom cubbies for people to find. She went dancing on weekend nights, when there were bands that played in the student center. She stayed up late talking with Stacey S, tie-dyeing T-shirts in the sinks.

But the sadness was still there, underneath.

Mikey Double L removed it a pretty large amount of the time. He just did.

He never failed to show up. He waited for Adelaide on the steps of the dining hall. He kissed her in public with big, firm smooches, like he felt very enthusiastic about her, and in private with a kind of glee, as if the two of them shared a fun secret.

They didn't sleep together, though they talked about it. It felt like they were always hard-pressed to find time alone—

before roommates got back, or before curfew, when everyone was required to be in their rooms.

And maybe they weren't ready.

They had been a couple for six and a half months when they decided to spend the summer together. Mikey's parents lived three hours away, but he could live in a teacher's guest room in exchange for doing some babysitting. He had a work-study job mowing lawns and tending plants that paid way better than what he could get back home.

"Let's both be here," he said to Adelaide. "Would you want to?"

Yes.

"All summer, having picnics on the quad, taking bike rides. What do you think?"

"Don't you want to see your parents?" she asked.

"I'd rather be here with you."

Adelaide and Mikey planned to meet up each morning after Adelaide had walked the dogs, in their favorite café in town, the one with the light wood floors. They would order almond croissants. And they'd be alone—alone for the first time, really. Without roommates or dorm supervisors, without homework, without friends who wanted to form study groups, play Frisbee, or commiserate. Nearly empty, the campus would spread out before them in the long summer days.

It was mid-June, the day before the end of spring term. Classes were over. Finals were over. The graduation ceremony was happening on the lawn. Students were packing to go home for the summer.

Mikey came to see Adelaide as she painted Levi's bathroom

a color called Adriatic Mist, a pale turquoise. He brought her a sandwich, the avocado grilled cheese she always ordered from Uncle Benny's Fine Sandwiches in town. She kissed him for it but didn't eat it right away. She went back to painting, because she wanted to get the edging done.

Mikey Double L sat on the floor of the hallway while she worked. He ate a banana and a meatball sub, drank a lemonade. He talked about his friend Aldrich, who was spending the summer in France on a youth program, and some guy he knew who was doing Outward Bound.

Adelaide didn't tell him about flunking Set Design. She hadn't even told him about academic probation.

Mikey finished his food and shoved the greasy white wrapper into the brown paper bag.

Mikey said, "I've been meaning to tell you."

What?

Mikey wiped his hands on his jeans and said, "I quit my job at the physical plant."

Mikey said, "I quit the babysitting, too, and told Ms. Sakata I wouldn't be staying with her."

Mikey said, "My mom signed me up for a service trip. Four weeks in Puerto Rico."

Mikey said, "Things haven't been the same between us."

Mikey said, "It makes me really sad, but I think this is the end."

Mikey said, "I've known this was coming for a while. It was just hard to face up to."

Adelaide felt dizzy and sick. She reached her hand out to steady herself on the wall, forgetting about the paint. "Yesterday we were in your bed together," she said, her voice sounding thin and quavery in her own ears. "Today you bought me a sandwich."

She said, "Why would you plan to spend the summer here, if you knew this was coming?"

She said, "You don't just fall out of love. Was it something I did? When exactly did you stop being in love?"

She could hear how pitiful she sounded. Her breathing was hysterical and shallow.

"Maybe I wasn't in love at all," said Mikey Double L. "Maybe I was in love with the idea of love. Maybe I wanted to be an ideal boyfriend. I wanted to make you happy."

She said, "You're leaving me here alone. I have dogs to walk. I can't leave them when there's no one to take them out."

She said, "I thought you loved me, because you said you loved me."

Mikey said, "I know. I'm sorry."

Mikey said, "I'm leaving later this afternoon."

Mikey said, "I hope we can be friends. I don't want to lose you."

Mikey said a lot of things, the things people say when they're ditching someone and want to soften the blow.

Then he said, "I still haven't ever been in love. It's not your fault, Adelaide. I don't think you've ever been in love either. We shouldn't waste our summer here, telling ourselves lies."

Adelaide tipped over the paint can when he said the word *lies*. She stood barefoot on a plastic tarp in a puddle of Adriatic Mist and humiliation.

How could Mikey tell her she had never been in love?

How could he say they hadn't loved each other when they had spoken those words aloud, in the dark and in the bright light of the cafeteria?

He was taking away her first love, taking it away, when it had been the good story, the only good story of her year at Alabaster, a story she thought she would remember her whole life: falling in love with Mikey Double L, simple and pure.

Mikey gathered up his lemonade and his backpack and the sweatshirt he'd taken off. "I'm sorry, Adelaide."

He walked up her dad's hall and out the door.

Adelaide ran after him, tracking paint.

She caught him in the yard, pulled him to her, and kissed him.

She kissed him with all her sad soul. She thought:
This kiss will
make him change his mind. It'll
make him feel
what I know he used to feel.

This is a grand gesture, she thought. *He cannot reject me when I am standing in my bare feet, covered in paint, on the lawn, for all the teachers in neighboring buildings to see.*

The kiss will draw him in.

Mikey kissed her back, but his kiss felt mechanical. She could tell he wanted it to be over.

7

A TERRIBLE SPIRAL

Adelaide couldn't bear to clean up the paint. There were footprints going down her father's hall and continuing onto the front steps. There were handprints on the door, but she didn't care. She left the roller lying in the tray and the brushes sitting out, still sticky. She left the jars open. None of it seemed to matter, since Mikey had stopped loving her.

It didn't matter how many
articles she had read about self-worth.
It didn't matter that
her parents loved her or that Stacey would stand by her,
because
the important person had turned cold, and
that was the person she had showed the most of herself to.
That was the person she got
naked with.

She thought back over the previous week. Were there a thousand clues she'd missed? Mikey had been late to meet her once. He had been slow to reply to a text. He had been busy a couple of nights with studying or working out or prepping for the photography club art show. But he had met her for lunch. He had stopped by her room to kiss her good night, right before curfew. He had held her hand at an end-of-year concert.

Adelaide left Levi's house, still covered in Adriatic Mist. She walked through campus, past the gym, some dorms, and the dining center, before she got to Wren Hall.

Mikey was probably upstairs in his suite that minute. Going about his Mikey Double L business and feeling relieved and even spectacular to be free of Adelaide Buchwald.

She wanted to see Mikey again, right now.

She wanted to take the

unresolved churning pile of shit that was in her mind,

the shit of being unloved and

rejected and betrayed,

the absolutely ugly shit that was Mikey's fault,

and she wanted to

dump it in front of his

door. He would open the

door and be shocked. He would say,

Is this really the shit that I have caused to blob up in the mind of the girl I love most in the world? What terrible shit!

He would take up the shit lovingly, literally pick it up in his arms, and he'd say,

Oh, I see it all now. I am the one who caused this shit to be so very shitty.

This shit is all my fault, and

thank you, Adelaide, for showing me this shit, because

it makes me feel quite amorous, actually,

to realize that the shit inside you (that is there because of me)
is actually this huge

(because the shit would be about the size of a laundry
basket), and he would say,

The shit proves that you are a deep and beautiful person,
because

only a deep person would have so much so very, very much shit
inside her as a result of me dumping her.

Come here, my love.

Let us run to the lake, where we will strip down and skinny-dip
together, washing off the terrible turds of betrayal and unhappiness
and never speaking of them again.

We will come out clean and lucky and remade.

I am so glad you showed me this shit.

Of course Adelaide did know that that is not what happens
when you show up at someone's door with a huge armload full
of your own shit.

She knew that, but

she went up there anyway.

Mikey's suitemate answered when she banged on the door.
"Double L isn't here. He went to get lunch with Sloane and
Reed."

"He just ate a sandwich, Aldrich," Adelaide said.

"I don't know. The guy could eat again, I guess."

"And he hasn't packed."

"Yeah, he kind of has. Why are you covered in paint?"

"Did you know he was leaving?" Adelaide pushed Aldrich on the arm. "Did you know he was going to Puerto Rico?"

"I'm an innocent bystander, Buchwald," said Aldrich. That was what he always called her. She had eaten lunch with Aldrich one hundred million times. She had gone to his parents' country house for a weekend, once, with Mikey and some other people. She had sat in the Nguyen family Jacuzzi and talked to him encouragingly about his crush on Tendai, who would never look at him.

"You're not an innocent bystander," said Adelaide. "You should have told me."

"Whoa. I definitely should *not* have," said Aldrich. "That is not my business."

"Let me in the suite."

"I don't think that's a—"

"Let me in the suite, I said."

"Fine, go in the suite," said Aldrich. "Knock yourself out."

Adelaide stood in Mikey's room, looking at his trunks, which would stay in storage at Alabaster until the following school year, and his suitcases, which would go home. His fencing equipment. He still had toiletries on his desk, but most of his things were indeed packed. His laptop was open and plugged in.

She had spent so many hours in this tiny space, feeling lucky to be there.

She would never be here again. This was the last moment.

Was there anything of hers, here, to take back? A book, a sweatshirt, even a pack of tissues?

There was nothing.

The Lego sculptures she'd made for Mikey were gone. They weren't in the trash either. The little drawings she'd made him weren't tucked into the mirror like they used to be. And they weren't in the bedside table drawer, where he sometimes kept them.

She was erased from his room.

Adelaide looked wildly for some mark to leave, some way to etch herself into Mikey's life. She could leave a painted handprint, but her hands were already dry. She could leave a note, but she couldn't bear the thought of him catching her writing it while sitting on the bed they'd been together on, only the day before.

Aldrich stood in the doorway, staring at her.

Finally, she snatched up a worn Alabaster Fencing T-shirt and left the suite.

8

THE EGG YOLK OF MISERY

The room Adelaide had shared all term with Stacey S was now an unimaginable mess. Adelaide was already moved into Levi's for the summer, but Stacey's belongings were everywhere, some of them halfway shoved into black garbage bags.

Stacey had a short, sharp way of speaking and almost no boobs. Her fashion sense centered on baggy jeans with lots of zippers and electrically bright tight-fitting T-shirts, a deviation from standard Alabaster wear. Her dad was a moneyed white guy from New Jersey who'd discovered yoga in his late twenties and become an instructor. Her mother was a Mexican-born artist who made ceramics. They ran a retreat center—like a B&B, but with kombucha and crystals—about an hour from school. Stacey was going home to work there for the summer, making green smoothies for people in the early mornings and vacuuming the rooms in the middle of the day.

Stacey went to Alabaster because her paternal grandfather had gone there and he paid for it, not because her parents valued that kind of thing.

Stacey looked at Adelaide. "Did something happen to Toby?" she asked.

Toby.

Of course that was what Stacey would think.

"No," said Adelaide. "Mikey stopped loving me."

"I was scared that might happen," said Stacey.

"He told me he never loved me and also told me that *I* never loved *him*." Adelaide started crying again.

"Oh, honey." Stacey hugged her. "Do you want cream soda? Will that help?"

"I need tissues." Adelaide sniffed. "And yes, cream soda."

"I'll get toilet paper," offered Stacey. She ran to the bathroom down the hall and came back.

Adelaide pulled a huge amount of paper off the roll and buried her face in it, sitting on Stacey S's bed. "What did you mean, you were scared it might happen?"

Stacey handed over a cream soda from the mini fridge. "I saw it coming."

"How?"

"Mikey is like, full of bonhomie. He's very positive about everything. He says yes to things when he doesn't really mean yes."

Adelaide popped open her soda. "I didn't say 'Let's spend the summer together' until he said 'Let's spend the summer together.'"

"He's the guy who says he'll do a project and doesn't do it," said Stacey S. "And he's the guy who says he'll be somewhere when he can't actually be there, because he doesn't want to disappoint someone. He always says yes, but he doesn't mean it, and people get jerked around."

"How do you know?"

"From fencing-team Tyler."

Adelaide sniffed. "Really? He never did that stuff to me."

"You were the priority. Mikey always put you above his other obligations."

That was exactly what Adelaide loved about him.

"He likes the idea of everything being great more than he likes seeing what's actually in front of him," Stacey S went on. "That's what I don't like about Mikey Double L."

"I'm not feeling any better from this conversation," Adelaide told her.

They sat on the floor with garbage bags all around, drinking their cream sodas. Each of them leaned against a twin bed. They played the board game Trouble, that one with a little plastic dome that you press down to roll the dice. Pressing it makes a horrible noise. Each time it popped, the sound felt like a punishment Adelaide deserved

for being pitiful when Mikey dumped her, for

crying and going all blotchy, for wiping her face with Adriatic Mist fingers,

for showing up at the suite and embarrassing herself in front of Aldrich,

for wanting someone who didn't want her,

for being secretly sad and obsessive about Toby all the time.

She was scared that Toby would relapse again.

That her mother was broken.

She was scared of the summer looming, the campus lonely.

"You're too good for Mikey Double L," said Stacey S.

"That's a thing you say when someone gets dumped," Adelaide told her. "It's a thing everyone says."

"But it's true."

"It's like he always knew we were only going out until the end of the school year."

"The school schedule is a major defining factor in relationships," said Stacey. "Remember how I went out with Catelyn One until Thanksgiving? But then you leave school, you eat some turkey, you feel disgusting, you watch movies with your relatives, your house fills with the smell of turkey soup, you feel more disgusting, you hate everybody, and then you think, *I should be happy to go back to school and see my lovely girlfriend, but now I don't even want a girlfriend. Life is all soup and movies and feeling like crap.* You realize the girlfriend isn't going to make you feel even one jot better with Christmas break around the corner, because you'll only even see her for three weeks, so you just break up with her by text, and it's such a relief. That never would have happened if we hadn't been sent home Wednesday to Sunday for a holiday about the colonial enterprise, screwing over the Wampanoag, gluttony, and waste."

"But didn't you already like Katelyn Two?"

"I liked Katelyn Two, but I liked Katelyn Two before I started going out with Catelyn One," said Stacey S. "I wouldn't have broken up with Catelyn One because of Katelyn Two. I broke up with Catelyn One because of Thanksgiving break, and I started going out with Katelyn Two the night before winter break, because somehow the last night of a term, everyone feels nostalgic, and you appreciate each other more, and you think, *Now we're all going off into the cold to engage in hot chocolate and peppermint sticks and relatives and what if I never see this cute Katelyn Two ever again? What if she gets hit by a bus? What if I get hit by a bus?* And so I kissed her because of winter break and then we went out until right before Valentine's Day, because that whole holiday, and the dumb dance they had in the Great Hall, put too much pressure on our relationship. That's why she dumped me five days before. I fully think that if there had been no Valentine's Day, I would be still going out with Katelyn Two. Damn it."

"You're too good for her," Adelaide told her.

"Yeah, but I still think about her."

"Valentine's Day isn't a school schedule thing."

"Well, you know what I mean."

Stacey hadn't had a girlfriend since Katelyn Two broke up with her.

"Am I ever going to not feel wrecked?" Adelaide said. "I feel like

ever since Mikey broke up with me at twelve-forty-five,

and now for possibly the rest of my life, there is an

invisible membrane

between the rest of the world and me, and it's an

ugly, slimy, viscous membrane,

like on an egg yolk but tougher, and

I won't be able to poke through it.

I will be stuck looking through the membrane to the life outside, in a terrible

egg yolk of misery."
"A membrane?"
"Yes!" Adelaide cried. "I am an
egg yolk of misery inside a
membrane,
and the name of the
membrane
is Mikey broke up with me."
"You are losing it," said Stacey S.

9

BACON IS
DEFINITELY MEANINGFUL

The morning after they went swimming, Jack showed up at the dog run. He was holding a paper bag stained with grease.

"Diner breakfast," he said. "Leftovers. I thought your dogs would like it."

Adelaide couldn't believe he'd showed up. After she'd taken the call from Mikey. She looked in the bag. "You had four leftover pieces of bacon?"

"Fine. I'm lying. I ordered it specifically. For you. It's to-go bacon, not leftover bacon."

The dogs were interested in the bag. EllaBella sat, docile and well-behaved. Everyone else circled expectantly, whining.

Adelaide took a bite of bacon. "I have to make sure it's not poison."

Jack laughed.

She distributed the bacon in small bits. The dogs took it from her hands with gentle mouths.

"Thank you," she said to Jack, after Rabbit had eaten the paper bag. "Cold bacon is a good present."

"I try to keep it classy."

The morning after they went swimming, Jack showed up at the dog run. He was holding a paper bag stained with grease.

"Diner breakfast," he said. "Leftovers. I thought your dogs would like it."

"That's sweet," said Adelaide.

She was thinking about Mikey Double L. How she'd wanted to talk to him on the phone more than she wanted to talk to Jack, even after the day of swimming they'd had. How she missed him. His voice in her ear, saying he was nervous to fly alone, worried about his Spanish, having done a terrible job packing—he had texted *her*. She was still the one he reached out to.

She held Jack's bag of greasy bacon as the dogs circled her. He had seemed so impossibly beautiful yesterday, but he seemed ordinary now. Just a cute-ish boy, with an unusual walk and a lazy way about him. Nothing beside Mikey's energy and industry.

Mikey needed her. Had missed her. And Adelaide would always love him.

The morning after they went swimming, Jack showed up at the dog run. He was holding a paper bag stained with grease.

95

"Diner breakfast," he said. "Leftovers. I thought your dogs would like it."

"That's sweet," said Adelaide.

"I wanted to say sorry," said Jack.

"What for?"

"I—I asked you out yesterday, and you know, I think we had a really good time. But when you took that phone call, I realized—"

"I shouldn't have taken that call," interrupted Adelaide. "That was rude. I'm sorry."

"That's not it," said Jack. "I realized I shouldn't be there. At the taco place. With you."

"Why not?"

"I have someone else," said Jack. "It's new. Just a couple weeks. But I think it's—well . . . it's a thing. I shouldn't have gotten distracted. I mean, you're a very distracting girl."

"I am." Adelaide forced herself to say it brightly.

"Yeah. And I'm kind of a jerk to have brought you out swimming when I'm not really free."

"Yeah. You are," she said. "But thanks for the intel."

"What diner did you go to?"

"That one on Fremont. I went for a six a.m. breakfast. I had trouble sleeping."

He looked at her water bottle, which was on the bench. "Do you mind?"

"Go ahead."

He drank.

She wanted to leap on top of him because he'd brought her bacon.

Maybe if she just leaped on him while he sat there on the park bench, Jack would be like, *Oh yeah, let's make out. That is why I brought the bacon, after all—to get you to make out with me.*

He really might. He was looking at her with the look of a boy who had taken a good deal of trouble to bring a girl an excellent and very greasy present.

"I had this boyfriend Mikey Double L," she told Jack. "He broke my heart abruptly. Recently. That's why I cried the other day."

"When did it happen?"

"Last week."

"Do we hate him forever? Should I embark on a campaign to avenge your wounded spirit?"

"I just might not be over it," Adelaide said. "I like you so much, and I might not be over it."

"The bacon doesn't have to mean anything," Jack said. "It's just a pork product."

"I'm just saying," she told him. "People befriend me because they think I'm

happy. I'm not even sure why they think I'm

happy, but they do. I get distracted, and

I laugh, and

I turn something on in myself that makes me, maybe, fun to be with.

And I'm just— I want you to know up front that I'm

false advertising.

I don't mean to be;

I just am. I have, like, this

huge misery inside me that's really very, very unattractive, and it has to do with my

abruptly broken heart but also with

my brother, who is messed up possibly beyond repair."

"I didn't think you seemed happy," said Jack.

"You didn't?"

"No. I thought you seemed interesting."

Adelaide didn't know what to say to that.

"I like listening to you talk," continued Jack. "You're surprising." And he reached out his hand to her. When she gave him hers, he

pulled her to him, fast, and they

stumbled a little, his leg making it a little hard for him to balance, apparently, and he kind of

caught her mouth with his, and his kiss was so

urgent, and so

sweet, that Adelaide felt she might

collapse with the

joy of it.

"Bacon is definitely meaningful," said Stacey S on the phone. "But it's no bicycle. And the bicycle turned out to be unimportant too, in the long run. Though I'm sure Mikey meant it at the time."

"I don't want to talk about the bicycle." Adelaide was sitting on EllaBella's stoop, scratching the dog's hairy neck.

"Okay, Adelaide, but there are lots of things you don't want to talk about. And yet, you're calling me." Adelaide could hear the whirr of Stacy's blender in the background.

"What should I do?"

"I think you should not go out with anybody right after breaking up with Mikey," said Stacey S. "I think you should work on yourself." The blender stopped.

"But with Jack, I feel things it took me months to feel with Mikey. He's, I don't know, spectacular. Necessary."

"Do you want me to see if my parents will let you come down and do yoga here?" asked Stacey. "I'm drinking kale right now. It's surprisingly okay. There's pineapple in with it. That's the key. You put enough pineapple in a smoothie and you could put, like, dog poo in there and nobody would taste it."

"Ick."

"You'd have to sleep on a blow-up on the floor, but you could probably take some yoga classes. You could drink kale and meet Camilla. It will help you get over Mikey." Stacey and her ex-girlfriend Camilla were dating again.

"I am absolutely over Mikey," said Adelaide.

"You're not over Mikey. I'm telling you that right now. It was a very big deal, you and Mikey."

"I am *over* him."

"*Not over Mikey* is written all over everything you're saying in this phone call."

"The question, more accurately," said Adelaide, "is how do I conduct this new relationship
   or possible relationship
   in some different, better way so that
   I'm not a secretly sad

not-all-the-way-lovable person, but am instead the
personification of self-actualized awesomeness
and will therefore get what I want, given that
what I want is
Jack?"

"You mean besides coming here to do yoga and drink kale?
Because that would self-actualize you."

"I can't leave the dogs. And yes, besides that."

"I don't know," said Stacey. "I think you're lovable and Mikey
Double L is just not that great, that's what I think."

10

THE ATTRACTIONS
OF TRAGEDY

That afternoon, Sunny Kaspian-Lee summoned Adelaide to
her studio classroom to talk about the missing project. One
section of the room featured four sewing machines and racks of
clothes—costumes from past productions. There was a closet
jammed with fabrics and props. On the other side were tall
tables surrounded by stools. Dirty box fans whirred on the floor
in a number of places, circulating the air.

Kaspian-Lee sat at one of the small tables. She wore a gray
dress of unusual architecture, plus a pair of pointy-toed flats
that made her feet look constricted and witchy. She did not
say hello.

"I need you to deliver on this project, Adelaide Buchwald. If
you don't, I'll have to fail you."

"I know. I'm sorry."

"I don't want to fail you. I'm a nice teacher. I want to teach you. But you've done very little work thus far, and if I weren't friends with your father, I would be flunking you like I would any other entitled kid who blows off my class."

"I've had a lot on my mind this term."

"That doesn't matter, I'm sorry to say. You still have to work."

"I will work."

"I need the *Fool for Love* project by August tenth. After that, my lover, B-Cake, and I are going to the seashore." Kaspian-Lee pushed over a printout of the assignment.

"My problem is the motel room," said Adelaide. "When I saw everyone else's models, they were, whatever, just that. Motel rooms. They all looked the same."

"That's not why you didn't do the work."

Adelaide felt herself flush. "No, it's not."

"People did some clever things," said Kaspian-Lee. "Listen. I assign this play because it requires only a single set. It's a good basic project. However, *Fool for Love* is not a naturalistic play. Read it, Adelaide Buchwald. I can tell you haven't read it."

Adelaide looked at the floor.

"What happens in this play is not everyday life."

"Okay," said Adelaide.

"All right. Now that you've had your talking-to, here's a key to the building and the classroom. That way you can work here, where the supplies are." Kaspian-Lee collected her bag from the table and headed toward the door.

"Wait," called Adelaide. "Is that guy Jack still walking B-Cake for you?" Just saying his name felt huge. She had been thinking about him all day.

"He told me he ran into you. At the dog run."

Adelaide's heart beat faster. "Is he walking her regularly?"

"No, he isn't," said Kaspian-Lee. "I get my lover, Martin Schlegel, to walk her. I am trying to get Mr. Schlegel to appreciate dogs, you see." She sighed. "It is an uphill road. B-Cake growls at him and farts in the kitchen. Martin doesn't appreciate either of those behaviors."

"Yes," said Kaspian-Lee. "I rather like having good-looking people do chores for me."

"What?"

"Don't be scandalized. Hetero men have enjoyed pretty waitresses and nurses for centuries now." She slung her bag over her shoulder and headed for the door. "Don't fret, Adelaide Buchwald," she said as she left. "Just build your model, serve the play, and pass this course. It's really not very difficult."

"Jack is not walking B-Cake at all. He's not a responsible walker of B-Cake."

"What happened?"

"He fed her dog biscuits. She isn't supposed to eat biscuits. I don't know why he even had them."

"That's so bad," said Adelaide.

"I know," said Kaspian-Lee. "Horrid digestive things happened."

Of course, it was Adelaide who had given B-Cake the dog biscuits.

Jack had lied to protect her.

"I've had very little business with Jack," said Kaspian-Lee. "He's not my concern. Don't mention him to Mr. Schlegel."

"What do you mean?"

The teacher took out a cigarette and lit it, even though there was no smoking allowed in the building. She opened a drawer and pulled out an ashtray. "Why do you think he's beautiful?" asked Kaspian-Lee. "Tell me."

"I didn't say he was beautiful."

"Anyone would say he was beautiful. What I'm asking is, why?"

"I don't know," said Adelaide. "His features are symmetrical?"

"No."

"His eyes are far apart?"

"Lots of people have wide-set eyes or symmetrical features. What happened to Jack's leg?"

"He was born that way."

"There's still a story. He's had surgeries. The point is, we want to know. But it's rude to ask. So there's a tension there. And not only the leg and the scars, but the dead mother, the time in Spain. There's the whiff of tragedy, and of experience. Tragedy is attractive."

"I don't think it's attractive at all," said Adelaide firmly. "Tragedy makes people compulsively sad and unlovable. It's like a dirty stain."

"Untrue. It's attractive on your father, for example. His hardship with your brother. It interests people. Tragedy . . ."

Attractive on your father.

Attractive on your father?

"Tragedy is a pinnacle of human experience," Kaspian-Lee went on. "Not that any of us wants to experience it, but we like to think about tragedy quite a lot. That's why Shakespeare wrote tragedies, and the Greeks. It's why we like *Fool for Love*— the doomed romance."

"I don't think you should be talking about students' beauty," Adelaide said to Kaspian-Lee. "Or my father's attractiveness."

"Jack is not my student," said Kaspian-Lee. "He's not matriculated at Alabaster yet."

"He's a kid."

"Oh, you're being very old-fashioned. I'm not going to touch that boy or interfere with him any other way. And I'm hardly going to bother with your father when he's happily married and I have Martin Schlegel." Kaspian-Lee extinguished her cigarette. "I'm saying all this as an artist and a human being. You hold on to everything very tightly in your body. Did you know that? I wouldn't be at all surprised if it made you ill one day soon. Loosen up, Adelaide."

And with that, she left the room.

11

I'M NOT TRYING TO MAKE YOU INTO SOMETHING YOU'RE NOT

Back in August, Toby had returned to the Baltimore house three nights before Adelaide left for Alabaster. He was beginning ninth grade over again at fifteen, going to the school Adelaide was leaving. He still had sober-living stuff he had to do each week: a group, a sponsor, a therapist.

Of course Adelaide had seen Toby since he'd moved to Future House. He'd been home for a few weekends. But they didn't know each other anymore. They didn't play Unstable Unicorns, or make up strings of swear words, or tease their parents together. None of that.

Toby was going to take Adelaide's bedroom. Adelaide and Rebecca had fixed it up for him. Rebecca knitted him an afghan. Adelaide took down her posters and drawings but left him her collection of cacti. Rebecca changed the bedding to Toby's old blue sheets.

When the car pulled up from Future House, Levi and Toby made themselves very busy unloading things and carrying them upstairs. Adelaide gave Toby an awkward hug. He smelled okay. Like Dr Pepper, which he must have been drinking in the car.

He still didn't know how to shave. He was heavier than he had been last time she saw him, the result of a new medication.

She showed him the redecorated room and explained how to care for the cacti collection. "They're yours now," she said. "I thought they'd help you feel at home." He said thanks, but he didn't seem to actually like them. She waited for him to notice his old box of Lego bricks and the row of original Lego landscapes she'd built that were still on top of the bookshelf.

He didn't seem to see them.

An hour later, when he was downstairs, Adelaide went back to the room. She picked up the Lego box and lugged it downstairs to the garage, where her stuff for Alabaster was waiting to be loaded into her father's car.

Fine, then. She would keep it for herself.

Toby had a new smartphone, and he spent the rest of the day on it a lot, adding games and setting it up. He took a long shower and came to dinner with his hair wet. He didn't talk much during the meal.

The night before Adelaide left for Alabaster, her mother made lasagna and her dad made ginger cake. Adelaide was already packed but she couldn't sleep, so she and Toby found themselves awake after their parents went to bed. She would spend the night on the living room couch foldout.

"Want to watch a movie?" she asked. Toby was staring at his phone, playing *Plants vs. Zombies*.

"Yeah, okay."

She opened her laptop. They sat in the kitchen. She picked *The Bourne Identity*, an action movie, and Toby said fine.

Adelaide wiped the crumbs off the kitchen table.

And got up to make a piece of toast.

And to put honey on her toast.

And to put the bread away.

She couldn't sit still, because she was leaving for boarding school the next day. And because it was strange, having Toby next to her. She looked at him to see if he would laugh or comment on the movie.

He didn't.

She said, "Did you watch a lot of movies at Future House?"

He shrugged. "A few."

"Like what? Were there any you were into?"

"Not especially."

"I signed up for a class called Design for the Theater at Alabaster," she said. "And so I've started to think about it when I watch a movie. You know? I was thinking that in movies the design is almost always

realistic. Or

naturalistic, is what I mean.

It looks like real life. The cars on-screen look like

real cars on a

real street. The lighting is supposed to look natural. But in a play, you can have a

gesture. You can gesture toward a street. It can be abstract."

Toby was still looking at the computer screen.

"In the theater," Adelaide went on, wanting him to understand why she found this so interesting, "your audience doesn't
expect things to look

real. Like, you can't have a

real car on the stage, anyway, can you? So instead, you make
something

obviously artificial. You just

create the feeling. And maybe the thing you make, instead
of looking

real, feels

true. Maybe

truer than real. Does that make sense?"

"Sure. Yeah."

"Do you get what I mean?"

"Yes, Adelaide. I get it, okay?"

"Sorry." She knew she was being talky, and she knew they
were watching *The Bourne Identity*, but she wanted Toby to
understand.

He was still looking at the screen.

Was he even listening?

Did he not care?

Finally, she snapped. "You have to figure out how to shave,
okay? Dad has to teach you."

"What?"

She said, "Before you go to school. Learn to freaking shave.
Your mustache looks terrible."

She said, "I mean, not that you have to conform to other
people's ideas of how you should look. You don't. You shouldn't.
Shaving isn't mandatory."

She said, "Sorry, that was dumb. Or insensitive. Something. I just— It's not my business how you look. I'm sorry. I'm sorry I said anything."

Adelaide felt herself spiraling into a turbulent mix of desperation and fury and love. "I'm leaving tomorrow," she said. "I don't want the last thing I said to you to be terrible stupidity about facial hair. I'm not trying to make you into someone you're not."

She knew that wasn't quite true, though. She would have liked Toby to be

definitely, permanently sober, and

she would have liked him to

look pulled together and to be

happy and to

make jokes and just to

be the Toby he used to be instead of this new, terrible, closed-off, damaged Toby.

But it seemed like the right thing to say.

"I love you and your facial hair," she said. That was true, oddly. "I'm sorry if I'm a rotten sister."

Toby fingered his wispy mustache. "To be honest, I hadn't even noticed it," he said finally. "I've been kind of living inside my head and not looking in the mirror."

He got up and went to the bathroom to see it. There was a long pause.

"It's studly," he called.

She followed him and looked in the mirror too.

"Don't you think?" Toby said. "It's kind of folk-singer-who-gets-laid-a-lot. Like, a guy who takes his guitar to parties and strums it in the corner. Girls come up and want to make out. It's a damn fine look, Adelaide."

"Toby."

"What? You said you love me and my facial hair. You said it." He smiled. Into the mirror.

"It's extremely ugly facial hair," she said. "But if you're proud of it and you want to look like a folk singer, then I support you and your nutjob aesthetic." *I support you* was something both their parents said a lot, ever since they had started family therapy.

"Thank you," Toby said, preening. "I plan on rocking this look all through ninth grade." He turned and headed back to the kitchen. He opened the fridge and got himself a seltzer.

"Just kidding," he said eventually as he threw himself back in his chair.

"Oh, thank god."

They watched the rest of the movie. Adelaide fell asleep with her head on the table. When she woke, Toby had gone off to bed.

The next morning, Adelaide and Levi left for Alabaster. They drove north, listening to podcasts. Adelaide began her junior year.

She played Ultimate Frisbee and went to a capella concerts. She made friends with Stacey Shurman. She met Mikey Lewis Lieu and fell in love.

And in November, Toby relapsed.

Yes.

All the work,

the anguish,

the money,

the therapy,

the lines on her mother's face,

the extra fifteen pounds on her father's frame,

and he relapsed. Her mother had realized Toby was high one night. Just knew it, suddenly, from his gait when he got up off the couch. Rebecca had asked him directly: "Are you on something?"

"No."

"Are you?"

"It's okay," he told her. "I've got it under control."

How could he think he had it under control? After all the therapy and group work and sober living, how could he actually say that?

Rebecca called Levi that night, and Levi waited for Adelaide outside Wren Hall in the morning, standing in a woolen coat with a hat pulled over his eyebrows and tears streaming down his cheeks. He hugged Adelaide and sobbed out the news. Then he told her it would be okay. They'd make it okay. Toby would figure out how to be okay.

Adelaide knew her father was lying. How could he know? It wasn't possible to know.

Levi left her at school. He drove to Baltimore, seven hours in the rain, and together he and Rebecca managed to get Toby back to Kingsmont the following week.

Adelaide told Stacey S, but she didn't tell Mikey. She didn't want to weigh down her first love with her family unhappiness. With Mikey, she wanted to be a shiny, bright girl.

So she became shinier, brighter, whenever he was around. And when he wasn't, she thought constantly of Toby. That sentence was on repeat in her skull: *My little brother is an addict.*

Toby was still at Kingsmont when Adelaide went home for winter break. She slept in her old room that was now his room, knowing he'd probably gotten high in there. She stalked around and kicked things that belonged to him. The room seemed contaminated, even though Rebecca had cleaned it and put Adelaide's old quilt on the narrow bed.

Eventually, Toby graduated from the rehab program at Kingsmont and returned to Future House to live for a while.

The Buchwalds had faith in this second go at rehab. Toby would stay clean, they said. He could, and he wanted to. The relapse was a setback. Lots of addicts had setbacks, but still, their overall movement was forward, toward recovery. The journey was never going to be easy.

But Adelaide had no faith anymore.

Toby came home again in April, but she decided not to be there for spring vacation. She was too disgusted and furious and creeped out to even try to talk to Toby. She went to Mikey's instead.

At the Lieus', people ate fresh apricots at breakfast and sat around at night watching baking shows. No one was high. People were normal and liked themselves; and they liked

Adelaide. They went to the mall sometimes in the afternoon, to run errands or get coffee drinks. Adelaide visited Mikey's old elementary school. She walked with him on the seashore in the evenings.

They found the swing set he'd loved as a little boy. Mikey kissed Adelaide as she sat on the swing, and she felt dizzy and off balance, with the whoosh of the ocean in her ears.

PART II

12

IT BEGINS WITH DOGS

The evening after Jack brought her the present of the bacon, Adelaide was back at the dog run. The Great God Pan came up, wagging. *You were kissing Jack this morning! I saw you.*

EllaBella came over and flopped on the ground. *I love you, Adelaide.*

Rabbit asked, *Would you throw a stick for me?*

So Adelaide threw a stick.

Pretzel asked, *Could I have a dog treat?*

And she gave them each a dog treat.

Tired of listening to podcasts, Adelaide took pictures of the dogs on her phone.

One of each. Face-on. She made squeaky noises and talked baby talk at them till they looked at the lens.

She figured she could try harder with her brother. The two of them texted, now and then, now that Toby was allowed to have a phone again. Adelaide would write, "Happy Spring!" or "Good luck on your finals!" And Toby would text back with a thumbs-up.

The thumbs-up just made her sad.

She edited the dog portraits. Cropped them. Did a little filtering. Then she texted them to Toby.

She wrote,

> Hanging out with these guys.
> Jealous?

An hour later, he sent back a thumbs-up.

She wrote,

> Hanging out with these guys.
> Jealous?

He didn't reply.
She texted the same thing to Jack.

> Hanging out with these guys.
> Jealous?

He didn't reply either.

She texted the photos to Toby:

> Hanging out with these
> guys.

He wrote back right away:

> Jealous.

She texted the pictures to Toby.
She wrote,

> I miss you, little brother.

She almost deleted it.
She almost didn't send it.
But then she did.
He wrote back:

> I miss you too, Adelaide.

13

THE INSIDE OF A MIND,
MADE WITH MIRRORS

Jack didn't show up at the dog run the next day. Or the day after. Or the day after that.

He didn't answer texts either.

"So he doesn't like you back," said Stacey S, on video chat.

"But he brought me meaningful bacon and then he kissed me."

"It's really okay, Adelaide. Not everyone is going to like you. I remember him from when he went here," said Stacey. "He was very short back then. Is he taller now?"

"He's gloriously tall. Well, medium height. Why would anybody kiss someone and then disappear?"

"I kissed Tendai and disappeared."

"Oh yeah. I forgot that."

"I literally hid from her one time in a supply closet," said Stacey. "I saw her around a corner and just ducked in there like a jerk. But I couldn't really disappear full-on because it was the school year. We had classes together and stuff. But I stopped looking her in the eye, didn't talk to her, avoided any group she was in, all that."

"But why?"

"The kiss was like an impulse," said Stacey S. "We were at a track meet. She absolutely smoked everyone in her four hundred heat, and she seemed magical, when she was running. I think I'm into people who are really good at something, you know? Talent. Or skill, is maybe what I mean." Stacey shoved a handful of cashews in her mouth. "We were all on the bus home and she and I ended up next to each other in a seat. So we talked. Then we walked back to Wren. It was a pretty night out, and honestly, I think I kissed her four hundred win, not her. And then the next day, when I saw her in the cafeteria, and she was toasting her English muffin, I was just like nope nope nope."

"She didn't do anything wrong?"

"She was just being Tendai. I don't know, spreading jam on a muffin. And I literally skipped eating and went straight to class so I wouldn't have to see her."

"Was she upset?"

"Yeah, I think so. But I just couldn't. I had no interest at all."

"But you should have talked to her, Stacey."

"Yeah. Well, I have guilt."

"Do you think Jack was kissing my metaphorical four hundred win?"

"Maybe. Did you have a metaphorical four hundred win?"

"No. Actually I had a meltdown about Mikey."

"Maybe he's one of those guys who likes a challenge. He liked you better when he didn't think he could have you."

"Oh, yuck."

"Some people are like that. Or maybe he likes damaged girls, realized you were basically functional, and took off to look for a more mentally unstable person."

"I'm damaged."

"Don't say it like you want to be damaged. Gross."

"Okay."

"You're not that damaged, Adelaide. You are, like, a loyal good friend, plus you had a seven-month relationship with Mikey Double L, which is super mature compared to most people we know."

"Seven *and a half* months. Me and Mikey."

"People who glamorize damaged other people are blech. If that's Jack's deal, you don't want him anyway."

"I don't like any of these answers," said Adelaide. "I prefer to think he got run over by a bus and that's why he disappeared."

"Yes!" said Stacey. "We can hope."

As the Jack-less days stretched into a week, and then another week, Adelaide began going back to sleep in the mornings, after running the dogs. She dozed in her shirt and underwear with the fan blowing on her legs under the thin sheet. She could feel the morning's coffee still pushing through her veins, but she sank into sleep with relief and gratitude.

At the Factory museum, in one of the outlying buildings, there was a new installation exhibit by a woman named

Caroline Ximenes titled "Where You Are Is Around Where You Are." Adelaide went with Levi on a Saturday afternoon.

Entering the exhibit, you walked into a long hall. It had black floors, and mirrors on both sides of the walls. The ceiling was very high. You could look at yourself, reflected over and over. The mirrors were hung with fairy lights. Tiny white bulbs on green wires. The lights reflected each other too; lights and then lights and then lights.

Step through a door and you found yourself on a balcony overlooking a
space that
stretched out
below and above you.
Staircases ran up and down the space. There were
mirrors across the
ceiling and the floor.
Furniture was bolted to walls, all of it
painted gold.
That gold furniture was
reflected in
mirrors along the walls, and in the
mirrors on the ceiling.
The undersides of the
staircases looked like
staircases too.

Adelaide dropped into this exhibit. Something was there, something about her
own life that she could not put words to. Suddenly, she didn't know
where the floor was, or

where the walls were.

The repetitions in the reflection offered no exit.

This wasn't a room you could enter or leave.

It was the inside of a mind, both

infinite and

constrained into repetition.

Maybe that was the point.

After looking at the installation, Adelaide and Levi ate lunch together at the Factory café. Adelaide ordered a cream cheese sandwich that came on date-nut bread. Levi had black coffee, kale salad, and spice cake.

"Ms. Kaspian-Lee is kind of inappropriate," said Adelaide. "She keeps talking about her lover. And how attractive people are. To me."

"Oh god, some people are like that," said Levi.

"Like what?" asked Adelaide.

"No boundaries, narcissistic."

"Isn't she your friend?"

"I think she's smart. She cares about the theater, and the school, and she tells good stories. She has a terrible boyfriend, though. And she gets on my nerves. Please keep that in the vault."

"Mr. Schlegel is terrible?"

"Yeah. Well, a little bit terrible. Not dangerous."

"Do you have any real friends?" Adelaide asked. "Here at Alabaster?"

"Maybe," Levi said, scratching his chin. "I like this guy Jeffrey who's head of admissions. He and I have played tennis a couple times. And I think the other theater teachers are fun. They're cliquey, though. And no one's here in the summer."

"Are you lonely?"

Levi nodded. "I should probably try to make some full-on friends, shouldn't I? Since we're going to live here for at least another year. And maybe longer. Mom and Toby could come up and live here after that. If Toby is, you know, able to go here."

"Friends would be good," said Adelaide.

"I might start with one," said Levi. "One would be a bite-size project."

Adelaide finally read *Fool for Love*. It only took two hours. The play was very sad and odd. It was about a couple, May and Eddie, who fell in love in high school and then broke apart for very good reasons—disturbing reasons—but now they can't stop circling each other, longing for each other. Torturing each other.

She started by googling sets that had been designed for professional productions.

A motel room boxed in by a neon sign.

A motel room with shredded ceilings and walls.

The bed on one side of the stage.

The bed on the other.

The bed in the center.

The room with one wall sliced open.

A raked stage.

A production in the round.

A patterned floor.

She read some articles about set design. She looked at designs for other plays she had read for school: *King Lear, Death of a Salesman, Fences, M. Butterfly, A Doll's House.* One set was nothing but a brown velvet room and a few chandeliers, no furniture at all.

She decided to make a motel room of solid gold. In it, May and Eddie,

those obsessive lovers, would live out their

toxic relationship.

The gold, she would tell Kaspian-Lee, *creates a mood of sensuality that is also somehow*

depressing.

Fake and cheap.

Underneath the weird gold motel room would be

a layer of dirt. The audience could see

skeletons in the dirt, and old tin cans,

things rotting.

Adelaide put the bed on the wall, literally on the wall,

impossible to sleep on but

symbolic—a place that would never be restful for May and Eddie, not ever. It loomed over them.

Okay, it was a little wild. But she hadn't seen it before. There was no way Kaspian-Lee would think she'd snatched an idea off the internet. She could cite influences from shows at the Factory, so she'd get through that part of the defense.

Day after day, as she gave up waiting for Jack to get in touch,

Adelaide lived a life of wood and cardboard. She squeezed paint from tubes into plastic ice cube trays.

She built a tiny four-poster double bed with a bare mattress and no blankets. She built tiny, cheap-looking table lamps that would hang, all wrong, from the ceiling.

Her life became this box she was building, a box to house a play about sad, obsessive love.

14

WHY STORIES MATTER

Texts. Sent on the eighth day Adelaide worked on her *Fool for Love* model.

Adelaide.

Toby.

Can I ask you a favor?

Adelaide didn't answer.

She was fine to send her brother cute pictures of dogs. That was just being a good sister. She did that kind of thing for lots of people: her parents, Stacey S, her other friends from school. She texted them something small to make them happy. A reassurance, or a joke, a gif, a photo, a good morning.

She thought of it like giving tiny gifts.
But she didn't want to do any favors for Toby.

Adelaide.

Toby.

Can I ask you a favor?

Of course.

She didn't want to be a bad sister.

Can you Venmo me some
money? For a present for Mom.
Just a loan.

. . .

. . .

Adelaide?

Adelaide.

Toby.

Can I ask you a favor?

What?

Can you Venmo me some
money? For a present
for Mom. Just a loan, of
course.

I love you too much to send
you money, Toby. No.

What do you mean?

Just no.

What the actual F,
Adelaide. It's for a present,
I swear. I'm going to start a
junior counselor job at this
gaming place. Then I'll pay
you back.

What do you want to buy
Mom? I'll order it online and
have it shipped to you. You
can give it to her.

I'm not sure exactly. I want
to surprise her.

. . .

. . .

It'd be easier if you could
just loan me the money
so I could go shopping. I
think maybe $200. I know
it's a lot. But I can pay you
back soon.

. . .

. . .

Adelaide, are you there?
$150 would be okay too.

She texted her parents.

Toby wants money off me.
You should call his sponsor.
And check his room and his
bag. And his pockets, if you
have to.

—————————

Sophomore year, Adelaide found her brother. In the bathroom.
She had come home to the Boston house on a Saturday

afternoon with sticky fingers and a stomach full of popcorn. She'd dumped her things on the couch and stripped off her jacket.

"I'm home."

No one answered.

She went to the kitchen, where Rebecca usually left a handwritten note. Sure enough, on the table it said *Yoga class, back at seven. Dad back seven-ish. Please press start on the rice cooker.*

Adelaide pressed start. She drank a glass of water. "Toby?" she called.

No answer. His bedroom was in the basement now. The room had small, high windows and a vinyl floor covered with a rug. They had moved him down there when he was nine and Adelaide didn't want to share with him anymore. The room was big, though it had a low ceiling and still felt like a basement. Toby had about a third of it devoted to Lego vehicles he'd made and refused to dismantle.

Adelaide went to the top of the basement stairs and called again. "Toby? You home?"

He didn't answer, so she figured he was out. She threw herself onto the couch and checked her phone. She was bored. She knew she should clean her room, but maybe she'd watch a movie and clean it later. Hmm. What movie? Maybe *Amélie*. Maybe *The Royal Tenenbaums*. She couldn't decide.

Adelaide got up to pee and pushed open the door to the downstairs bathroom, the one Toby used.

There he was. And a needle on the floor.

He was hardly breathing.

132

Maybe not breathing.

Maybe not breathing.

Toby was slumped against the shower stall, awkward, as if he'd fallen off the toilet. Limp. He wore an orange-striped shirt that made him look like a little boy. He didn't have shoes on, and his white sweat socks looked bright and new. His eyes were closed and his mouth was open, blueish. He was wheezing.

Adelaide shook his arm. "Toby!"

He didn't wake. His arm felt like there were no bones in it. She touched his face and neck, feeling for a pulse. It was there, but the beat didn't seem normal.

She fumbled for the phone in her pocket. Called an ambulance. "My brother," she kept saying. "My brother, my brother." The dispatcher said help was on the way.

God. Toby still had a stuffed panda in his bedroom. He read books about Dungeons and Dragons. He still wanted to know if they could get a dog. Asked for leftover cake for breakfast.

Adelaide waited for the ambulance, seven long years. A hundred years.

Toby's lime-green electric toothbrush lay on the vanity. The cap was off the toothpaste. Hair gel, acne cream, deodorant— nothing had its top on, actually. His shampoo and body wash lay on their side in the shower stall, the washcloth wet on the floor.

Adelaide kept her fingertips on the spot underneath Toby's ear, feeling for a pulse that was soft and uncertain. She couldn't sense her body at all, though she was kneeling on the hard floor. She could only feel her fingers against that fragile pulse.

The EMTs rang the doorbell. She ran to open it. They

bustled in, a man and a woman wearing thick belts and uniforms.

Adelaide pointed to the bathroom and they didn't ask many questions. They booked it through the living room.

Somehow the running made it all seem real.

They needed to *run*. The few seconds they'd save were seconds that might save Toby's life.

Adelaide watched as they bent over her brother. The man gave him an injection. Then there was a pause. All movement stopped. They were waiting.

Toby's eyes flickered open.

"Okay then, yep," said the woman.

"Good news," said the man, looking at Adelaide.

They loaded Toby onto a stretcher. They took him out the door.

Adelaide called her parents. She couldn't say the word *overdose*. She couldn't say *drugs* or anything like that. She just said Toby had stopped breathing right, and his heart rate was weak, but the EMTs had come and he was okay now. She was going with him, in the ambulance, to the hospital.

There is a universe in which Tobias Morrison Buchwald died that day.

Adelaide never got up to pee. Instead, she watched a movie. She found him too late.

The family sat shiva and the neighbors brought fruit baskets, casseroles, and bottles of wine. Adelaide's friends,

Ashlee and Veronica, and her short-term boyfriend Mateo, sat in her bedroom while the friends and neighbors milled around the house, talking in grave voices. The four of them ate thick, powdery Italian cookies with jam inside. They listened to music and talked about how great Toby had been, shared funny memories they had of him.

The Buchwald family remained in Boston. Levi continued teaching public school and going to conferences, writing his book about Shakespeare in the curriculum. Rebecca kept her yarn store, teaching classes and working through her grief with intensive therapy. Adelaide spiraled into guilt and nearly unresolvable fury, but she did it in the heart of her family, with friends she had known most of her life.

She never met Ling and Joelle, never called Baltimore home.

She never went to Alabaster.

She never met Jack Cavallero or Mikey Double L, and therefore

never fell for either of them.

She was a Boston girl, a public school girl, a girl so steeped in sadness that no antic charm or easy distractibility developed to compensate for the milder sadness and worry that was her personality as we know it.

But also, the worst had happened. Toby was dead. This Adelaide didn't carry around the fear for him, the dread *of* him, that haunts her in other possible worlds, and that she works so hard to conceal.

There is also a universe in which Tobias Morrison Buchwald
   never
   got pulled along to parties with senior girls at all.

He said yes, early in his freshman year, to a skiing trip with
a friend from middle school,
   a trip he didn't really want to go on. He wasn't much of a
skier, and this friend and he were growing apart.

But he did go, out of obligation to this old friendship, and
he broke his collarbone on a downhill slope.

High school is a place where a neck brace can be the difference between people finding you adorable and the same
people finding you unworthy of their notice.

Toby fell immediately off the radar of the girls who had
been so charmed by him and instead found himself gaming
on Friday nights with a crew of ardent nerds who taught him
to master the Rubik's Cube.

His vulnerable brain chemistry did lead him to depression and self-loathing during his ninth grade year. It was
a bleak time. But one of his friends spoke up, and Toby's
parents were able to get him therapy and eventually, some
medication.

He still became a stranger to Adelaide. She reached out,
and he didn't respond.

She reached out again, and he didn't respond.

But they were there in the same house, together. They ate
dinner together, most every night. One day, when Adelaide
was a junior and Toby was a sophomore, she found him
rebuilding his old Lego airport and sat down next to him. She
used random bits from the Lego bin to make a diorama of

the pool at their YMCA. "This is Mom." She put the Poison Ivy Lego character into the pool. "And this is Dad." She put a postal worker. "This is me." She put Wonder Woman. "And this is you." She put the Joker.

"I want to be Harry Potter," said Toby.

"Okay, bring it on. Can you find him?"

Toby found Harry Potter. They put the four characters into the swimming pool together.

"Do you want to eat some butter and brown sugar?" said Toby. It was a thing they used to do when they were younger.

"I don't think it'll be as good as it used to be," said Adelaide. "But sure."

They cut a stick of salted butter into eight small squares and sprinkled brown sugar on each square. It wasn't too bad.

Texts. Sent three hours after she ignored his first set of texts on the subject, on the eighth day Adelaide worked on her *Fool for Love* model.

Adelaide.

Toby.

I still need that favor. Can you text me back?

Please?

. . .

. . .

. . .

Adelaide?

What do you want?

There's a girl I like. Darcy.

. . .

. . .

And what do you want?

Advice, I guess.

That's the favor you want?

Yeah.

. . .

Okay. Did you shave your
mustache? That is the first
step toward getting any girl
interested in you, Toby.

My mustache is ancient
history.

        Does she know you exist?

She is a junior counselor at
RPG day camp with me.

        You're ahead of the game,
        then.

It's just. Agggggghhhhhhhh.

        What's she like?

Hmm. She goes to a
different school from me.
Doesn't drink or anything.
She likes the campers. They
make her laugh so hard she
loses it and can't talk. Um,
what else? Blue stripe in
her hair. She's black. Good
at strategy games. Cool
handwriting. She makes all
these posters for camp. She
seems, I don't know, she
seems like she likes herself.

K.

So what I think is, you see her.

That's what I think people
want. Romantically.

They want to be seen.

This guy I've been going
out with—or was going
out with—maybe still—
Anyway—

He sees me. And he let me
know.

Do that, and I bet she likes
you back.

I was hoping you'd just say
something like make sure
to brush your teeth.

Make sure to brush your teeth.
That's actually crucial.

Noted.

Oh, try bringing her some
bacon.

Bacon, seriously?

Yes. Seriously.

Good luck.

Texts. Two days later.

Adelaide.

Toby.

Do you remember the
Halloween when Mom and
Dad ate all our Snickers?

Yes.

They had to buy a whole
bag of them to make it up
to us.

Yes. OMG.

Do you remember our
zucchini battle?

141

Mom was so mad because she had guests coming over and she was supposed to make ratatouille.

But yeah. It was epic.

Also you stuck that Tic Tac up your nose.

Minty! Terrible minty!
That's what I kept yelling.

Why would you do that? Every kid knows not to put something up your nose. It's like, a thing people tell kids, all the time. Don't put stuff up your nose.

I am a person whose character flaw is that he sometimes tries new experiences that are VERY BAD IDEAS.

. . .

. . .

Sorry. Too early for jokes?

Maybe never is a good time for
jokes on that subject.

Sorry. Sorry. You know, I
had a fear of Tic Tacs after
that.

You did?

I had to go to the hospital!

Don't be a baby. It was just
urgent care.

I still won't go near them.
Nasty little things.

Ha.

We should have another
zucchini battle someday.
Next time I see you.

. . .

. . .

Adelaide didn't answer him, this time.

She didn't want to start making plans with Toby. It was much too early to trust him.

Can I be serious for a minute?

Okay.

When I was at Kingsmont
the second time, everything
was very bleak.

It sucked to be back.

And the very annoying (but
also sometimes helpful)
group therapy leader said

Think of your happy
memories. Know they are
still in you.

They are part of you.

And maybe even they ARE
you.

It was corny.

Well, just a little.

What I mean is,

the Halloween candy story
is inside of us both. And the
zucchini. And the terrible
minty.

15

IDENTITY IS RARELY FIXED

One Friday evening, Adelaide went to the Factory on her own to see an exhibit titled "Also Known As."

The artist, Danitra Solo, had blown up false identification documents to enormous sizes. Various passports, driver's licenses, and student ID cards were printed ten feet tall on canvas. They looked pixelated to the point where you could only recognize the photographs as people when you stood back and squinted. Text on the wall said that all of these items were copies of fake documents Solo had acquired through extensive research.

In the corner of the room, a man with a handlebar mustache sat at a desk. A sign on the desk read "Identification."

"I'm available to make you a document," he told Adelaide when she approached.

He asked her to take things out of her wallet. "These are the paraphernalia of your identity," he said.

Besides her student ID and her bus pass, Adelaide's wallet held punch cards for the coffee shop and the bubble tea place, some money, a receipt from the drugstore, a receipt for the tacos she'd eaten with Jack, a vintage-store receipt, two gum wrappers, and the poem Jack had written when she met him two years ago.

She unfolded the poem and showed it to the man with the mustache.

> *Cerulean dress and*
> *wide eyes, like a lion.*
> *A raging wave of disobedient hair.*
> *She contains*
> *contradictions.*

"Someone loves you," he said. "Or admires you very much, at least."

She wasn't at all sure that was true, but looking at the poem reminded her that it had been true, once. Jack had seen her, briefly, at least. Really seen her. The poem was proof.

The man surveyed the bubble-tea card, the gum wrappers, and so on. "These are items that constitute some of your experience," he said. "Therefore, they constitute some portion of your identity."

He placed her items on a scanner and scanned them.

Adelaide waited in silence.

He took the items out of the scanner and returned the originals to her. She crumpled her receipts and shoved them in her pocket.

He took a plastic card with rounded edges and affixed the

pattern from the gum wrappers onto it as a background. Then he worked with an X-Acto knife to cut out a phrase from the poem Jack had written her. He put the words in the space where a picture would be. Instead of her face, it read *wide eyes, like a lion.*

He cut the word *healthy* from the bubble-tea punch card. From the taco receipt he took her name, which was listed there so the counter guy could shout it when her order was ready. From the coffee punch card he took the word *free*. From the vintage-store receipt, the word *felt*. From the drugstore receipt, the word *Twix*.

"Now you're just getting random," she told him as he pasted *Twix* onto her card with the other words.

"You carried this Twix receipt around with you," he said.

"Not on purpose."

"It was with you."

"I like that you put *free* on there," she said.

"Thank you," he said. "Do you think it needs anything more to function as your identification?"

"I don't know the answer to that," Adelaide said.

"That's all right, then," he told her. "I'll just laminate it."

He ran the new ID card through a laminating machine, trimmed it and gave it to Adelaide. "You're a new person now, in some small sense."

"Is this your job?" she asked him. "What will you do when the exhibit closes?"

"It's one of my jobs," he answered. "But I have others."

16

WHAT THE LIGHT DOES
TO THE CANVAS

Adelaide came out of the exhibit at nine-thirty p.m. to find her bike was gone.

The bike Mikey Double L had given her. Someone must have cut the lock.

She stood with her helmet in her hands.

It was raining.

She called her father. Levi didn't pick up. She remembered he was going to dinner with some people from the admissions office.

The taxi app said it would cost twenty-five dollars to ride back to Alabaster. Because of the drizzle, and it being Friday night, there was surge pricing.

Adelaide decided to walk. It would be fine. She left the Factory campus following a cobbled path, past a sculpture garden lit for the evening with glowing pink light, through a cluster of old brick buildings to the tall iron gates.

She wore her bike helmet to keep the rain off her head. And to avoid carrying it. Besides that, she had on a thin cotton shirt and a red knee-length skirt, plus a thick cardigan for the vicious air-conditioning in the Factory. Vans with black and white checks. No socks.

The Vans had been fine, but now they started to blister her feet.

Her backpack had been fine, but now it hurt.

Her phone said the walk was sixty minutes. She made her way through the run-down Victorians at the edge of town to a long main road that didn't have sidewalks.

A car pulled up next to her and stopped.

She picked up her pace.

The window on the passenger side slid down. "Adelaide."

She stopped. Squinted in the dark.

It was Jack.

Jack!

She had conjured him here. When she really needed help, he drove up in a Volkswagen, wearing a white T-shirt. "Adelaide, are you okay?"

"Someone stole my bike."

"Bastard."

She got in. She took her helmet off. She worried about her hair. Her clothes were soaked.

It was hard to breathe, Jack was so beautiful. His silver rings glinted in the streetlight. He was wearing glasses with black rims. She hadn't seen him wearing glasses before. "Where you coming from?" she asked.

"Playing poker with the guys from Uncle Benny's."

"Terrance and Oscar?"

"And some others. Where were you?"

"The Factory. It's open late on Fridays."

"How was it?"

"My favorite place in the world. Did you win at poker?" she asked.

"No, Oscar won, mostly," he answered. "That guy is a beast. But we're only talking about ten dollars or so."

Adelaide was so attracted to Jack, she had trouble concentrating on what he was saying. She was conscious of his body in the driver's seat, the way he moved when he flicked on his blinker or adjusted the heat.

She looked at his hands on the wheel. The car smelled faintly of doughnuts, sugary.

"What did you see?" he asked.

She brought her mind back. At the Factory. He was asking about the Factory.

She didn't want to tell him about the ID, because she didn't want to explain his poem being in her wallet, so she told him about a show she'd seen the previous week. "There's this woman who paints huge canvases with reflecting paint—like, the paint they use to put white stripes down the middle of the road. The light plays across them and seems to move."

"What does she paint?" he asked.

"No pictures of anything. Just paint. The idea is that the meaning isn't *on* the canvas so much as it's *in* what the light does to the canvas."

Jack nodded. "That's the kind of thing I want to be doing. I mean, I want the meaning of a painting to lie in the interaction of the image with the viewer."

"Your church hippo."

"Did I tell you about my pictures?"

Of course he had. The first time they'd met. He'd talked about them in some detail. It bothered her that he didn't remember. "A little," she said.

"It's not a church hippo."

"What is it, then?"

"Well, it *is* a church hippo, but it's also a car," he said. "The car part is very important."

"I'll remember that. If I get to see it, ever."

They pulled up in front of Levi's house. Jack turned off the Volkswagen. He didn't idle it. He turned it off. Then he turned and touched Adelaide's face,

---

leaned in and kissed her. She leaned into him too, reaching over to grasp his hand, feeling a wave of longing for him surge through her body. She ran her fingers up his chest and felt the warmth of his skin through the thin fabric. She felt shaky and strong at once, and she marveled at how a kiss could make a pair of bodies feel like the center of the universe.

Jack's phone buzzed. He pulled away. Dug the phone out of his pocket and glanced at a text Adelaide couldn't see.

Then he wrote back, quickly, and hit send.

"I have to go," he whispered. "Sorry."

Adelaide leaned in and kissed him again. Willing him to stay. Willing him to see her, and to want her.

"I wish I could," Jack said, his lips on her neck. "But I can't."

---

leaned in and kissed her.

Adelaide had wanted to kiss him since that moment of being in the hammock. She had longed to run her fingertips across his abdomen, to press her lips against his and to feel his breath against her cheek.

Only, now that it was happening, she couldn't stop thinking about how she was a physical mess.

Her hair was frizzy from the rain and squashed from the helmet. Her sweater was wet. It made a damp wool smell that filled the car. She wore an unattractive beige bra, because with her white T-shirt, anything else would show through.

Her mouth tasted slightly of the everything bagel with scallion cream cheese she had eaten at five-thirty instead of dinner.

She hadn't shaved her legs.

Did other people think about this stuff when someone kissed them? Or was it just Adelaide, running through a catalog of all the small unpleasantnesses she might be visiting on the other person?

You would think that since she wanted to kiss him so badly, she wouldn't think about anything else. Instead, she cataloged what Jack's experience might be and whether it would be a good one.

Of course she knew that Jack himself would probably have a more pleasant experience if she actually engaged full throttle in the kissing. Regretting the scallion cream cheese was not actually going to make her mouth taste any nicer.

He pulled away. "Something's wrong, isn't it?"

"No, no."

"Are you sure? I don't want to— Let's not do anything you don't want to do."

She wanted to do everything.

Everything.

But she couldn't. Because

Mikey didn't love her. Because

Toby was an addict. Because

of the scallion cream cheese and the ugly bra and the wet sweater smell,

because of the egg yolk of misery, basically,

Adelaide couldn't be present, in this car, with this magnetic boy.

"I should just go," she said.

She hated herself and

she hated the insecurity that made her hate herself and

she hated Jack for making all of that come to the surface.

———————————————

leaned in and kissed her.

"Wait," she said. "Wait."

"What?"

She folded her arms and pulled away. "You disappeared

for more than three weeks, Jack. Which you're allowed to do. Of course. But then—well. I don't think you get to do *this*, next time you happen to run into me, if you disappear."

"I didn't disappear. I've been working at Uncle Benny's. Painting. I didn't go anywhere, Adelaide."

"You know what I mean. I haven't heard from you. Since the bacon."

He touched her hair. "I was just busy, that's all. I'm so glad I found you there, on the side of the road."

She shook her head.

"I didn't mean anything by not being around," he added.

But she knew he did. She could see the future like it had already happened: Him disappearing again after kissing her tonight. Her missing him on top of missing Mikey and Toby.

"Thank you for the ride," Adelaide told him. "I really do appreciate it."

She got out of the car.

———————————————

leaned in and kissed her.

It was like she remembered from the dog run. His kiss wasn't cozy and conspiratorial like Mikey's but hungry and somehow appreciative, filled with longing.

She ran her hands through his hair and it was soft and fine, despite all the waves, and Adelaide felt the

rush of the party on the rooftop whiz through her, the beauty of the poem he'd written, the

poem that was now part of her identification. She felt she

knew him and loved him already, somehow, and also that

all the wonderful unfolding of their new love was just ahead of them.

Her phone buzzed in her pocket. It was her father. "Won't be home till after midnight. Watching *Henry V* with Matt Kwan from the drama dept."

Jack kissed her again, slowly moving his hands down her body until she felt like she could think of nothing else but this moment and the box of condoms she had bought, thinking she and Mikey would use them this summer, still unopened.

"Do you want to come upstairs?" she whispered.

"I do," he said.

They held hands as they went into the house. They fell dizzily, as they kissed, onto the folded-out bed. The rain ceased and the stars glistened outside the window. The sound of their own breathing was in their ears. Jack's hands were on her skin, gently and sweetly. The box of condoms got opened. He asked her what she wanted to do and it was awkward to talk about, but her answer was clear.

17

SOUL MATES AS A
GENERAL CONCEPT

In the morning, Adelaide felt bouncy and super aware of her surroundings. She made herself a big thermos of sweet milky coffee and walked the dogs in the gorgeous fresh summer day.

Stacey S arrived that afternoon to stay for two nights. She had four beers in her duffel bag. She had taken them out of her parents' fridge when they weren't looking. The beers were warm, but that evening Adelaide and Stacey drank them out in the soccer field, sitting in the middle of the green. They had a jumbo bag of Doritos and some store-bought guacamole. It was their dinner.

"I don't think more love is the answer," said Stacey, when she had heard about Jack.

"*You* have love," said Adelaide.

"It's not love, it's just summer *like*. But also, I had no love from Valentine's Day till school got out. I was a solo Stacey for like, four months. It was very good for me."

"It isn't good for *me*," said Adelaide.

"What's so great about Jack?" Stacey lay down on the grass and put a chip in her mouth.

"Everything. Solidly everything. It's like I knew him before," said Adelaide. "I mean, I did meet him before, a long time ago, but I mean, it's like I knew him in another life. In a parallel universe, or before we were reincarnated or whatever."

"Do you mean like soul mates? Because I'm not on board with soul mates as a general concept."

"Of course not," said Adelaide.

But that was what she meant, precisely.

"I hope you're not making this into a giant thing because of doing it," said Stacey. "The whole idea of virginity is just a sham tool of the patriarchy anyway." This was something Stacey had said before. She said there needed to be some better way to measure experience than virgin/nonvirgin because that crap didn't apply to lesbians the same way and also actually, it was fuzzy and confusing even for hetero people. And why were we measuring experience anyway?

"I'm not," said Adelaide. "It was a giant thing before that. It's a giant thing for other reasons."

Stacey stood up. "I wonder if he'll remember me. Let's text him."

"Now?"

"Yeah, now."

"I can't just text him the next day. I'll lose all my mystery."

"Oh my god, this isn't 1952, Adelaide. Text him."

"I totally have texted him lots of times. He just didn't text back."

"He will *now*. *Now* he's realized he's super into you. Also, there is like, nothing to do in this town. He's probably sitting at home with his father, bored out of his mind right now. He barely knows anybody. He'll be SO GLAD we texted him."

"Fine."

She wanted to text him anyhow.

Jack met them on the soccer field. He loped across it and threw himself down on the grass. "I brought an offering." It was a bag of gingersnaps. "It was all we had in the house."

"It's perfect," said Adelaide.

"Gingersnaps are my jam," said Stacey amiably. "Are you nervous about starting back at Alabaster?"

"Kind of."

"I'll clue you in to the terrible people," said Stacey. "Most people turned out pretty decent, but there are a few seriously terrible human beings, and you'll find it useful to have a heads-up. Also, don't eat the chili in the cafeteria, in case you don't remember that from before."

They decided to take Jack's car to Luigi's in Lowell, the next town over, where there was a pinball machine. They weren't hungry, but the soccer field was boring.

Luigi's was open twenty-four hours. Counter service. Garlic knots and calzone. Jars of powdery Parmesan on every table. A

TV set on one wall. There were a number of people clustered around the pinball, so Adelaide, Stacey, and Jack ordered a pizza and slid into a booth.

"Hey, hey."

It was Oscar the piano player. He sat down next to Jack. He was taller than Adelaide remembered, really very tall, and his black curls were unruly. His weight suited him, she thought. His cheeks were flushed in the heat of the pizza place and he had a bright energy about him that contrasted with Jack's laid-back way. He grinned and looked at Adelaide. "I owe you a beverage. Some water, anyway."

Adelaide laughed.

"I know Oscar from Uncle Benny's," said Jack, explaining to Stacey.

"I take orders up front," said Oscar. "Jack does stock and busboy stuff. It's a brutal scene. You can't imagine."

"Like what?" asked Stacey.

"He's making it up," said Jack. "Nothing's brutal."

The horde of pinball players heard their order number and rushed to collect their pizza and sit down. Stacey bolted up and got the machine.

"I'm going to get quarters," said Jack, motioning for Oscar to let him out of the booth.

Oscar did, but he didn't go sit with the people he'd been with before. Instead, he slid back in across from Adelaide. "He loves pinball," he said, about Jack.

"Oh really?"

"He's good at it. I don't know, maybe it's popular in Spain or something. I was serious about the beverage. Do you want a Coke?" said Oscar.

"Diet Coke," said Adelaide.

"Weirdo," said Oscar.

He got up and ordered sodas, then came back and set them down. Then he went to watch Jack play.

Adelaide realized that if they wanted to hold on to the table, one of them had to sit there. She watched Stacey, Jack, and Oscar screaming over whatever was happening in the pinball machine. She looked at her phone.

When the pizza came they returned to the table, flushed and happy. Oscar sat down with them as if there were no question at all that he was welcome, although he didn't eat their pizza. Adelaide put her arm around Jack's shoulder, glad that he was back. She tried to relax into the evening.

Terrance showed up and squeezed into the booth next to Stacey. He did eat their pizza. Oscar scolded him for being late. Terrance said Oscar was being an old woman. Stacey said that was a sexist insult.

Oscar, Terrance, and Stacey talked about college applications, and Adelaide felt the familiar swell of anxiety that came over her whenever the subject came up. Jack started writing on the napkins.

She plays pinball with guts
Although she isn't good at it.
She doesn't need to win at everything.
People look at her anyway.

He showed the napkin to Adelaide.

She took the pen from him and wrote: *Stacey?*

Of course, he wrote back. The next one said:

He eats pizza like he's
Never eaten pizza, like he's
Just discovering it. Like he can't believe
His luck.

Jack passed this one over to Terrance. Terrance picked it up and smiled.

"I wanted to go to music conservatory for high school," Oscar was saying to Stacey. "I applied for eleventh grade and again for twelfth, but I keep getting wait-listed and not *in*. I'll try again for college, but part of me has to face up to the idea that the height of my piano achievement may be playing holiday carols in shopping malls or teaching little kiddos how to play Minuet in G. It's unlikely I'll be a concert pianist, but I do need to keep trying for a while longer, see if I get a breakthrough or whatever."

"I have this college spreadsheet with columns for things that are important to me," said Stacey.

"Oh, ugh. Yuck," said Terrance.

"It's cool. Like, I have a column for film production classes. Lots of schools don't offer film production. Maybe you could look for places that have great music programs that aren't, like, conservatories?" she said to Oscar.

"I just want a big school," said Terrance. "State school, probably. More people. More kinds of people."

"How come?" asked Stacey.

"This small town is the death of me. I'm almost dead. Look at me. Feel my pulse. I'm literally bordering on dead from being here."

"Aw," said Jack. "But you have us now. And you have Uncle Benny."

The rest of them kept talking about college apps and Jack wrote:

> *The pianist is a performer. He is*
> *performing, now. For*
> *all of us. Even though there is no piano in the room.*

He shoved the poems for Oscar and Stacey across the table.

Oscar read his silently, then folded it and put it in his pocket. "Thank you."

"I am *too* good at pinball," said Stacey. "I was just warming up."

This time, they all five went to the pinball machine. Stacey was terrible but insisted she was amazing. Terrance was terrible too. Adelaide did all right, and so did Oscar. Jack was excellent, keeping the ball in play and touching the edges of the machine lightly, never banging it or using the flippers when he didn't need to.

Adelaide watched his hands. And his face as he concentrated.

She wanted him to write *her* a poem. Of course she did.

She knew she had one already, but that was from years ago. It seemed unfair that he would write for everyone but her.

At the end of the evening, Terrance got picked up by his mom, and Oscar squashed into Jack's car with them. He had taken the bus. Jack dropped Adelaide and Stacey first. "I'll see you soon," he said to Adelaide, though he didn't kiss her.

Well, it wasn't like they were a couple yet. And not everybody was in the Mikey Lewis Lieu school of public affection.

"Is he nice to you, Adelaide?" said Stacey as the two of them lay in the foldout bed, their teeth brushed and Adelaide's hair in braids to keep off the heat. "That's what I care about. If he's nice to you."

"I think so."

"I mean actively nice. Besides the bacon. I couldn't quite tell, is all. He was like, talking to Oscar all the time in the car. Does he make you happy?"

"It's not happy so much as a thrill," said Adelaide.

18

SHALL WE PRETEND
I WAS NEVER?

Texts.

Talking to our mom is
exhausting.

Yeah. Always.

But why today?

The anxiety. It's killing me.

When I talk to Mom I feel like
I have one job: to make her
happy by demonstrating that I
am happy.

Is that what you mean?

Yes. But on top of that I
have to perform sobriety.

                    Explain?

I walk straight lines, just
casually, while I tell her
what I did at school. I invite
her into my room to talk so
she can look around.

I end up being all

CHIPPER!

During the school year
I came home from
basketball and I'd say
HELLO! SCHOOL WAS
EDUCATIONAL AND
MY FRIENDS ARE NICE!
I WILL TAKE A SHOWER
AND THEN SET THE
TABLE. HOW WAS YOUR
DAY?

                    You played basketball?

Yeah. JV.

That's cool.

But I'm the same way with
the coaches.

SHALL WE PRETEND I
AM NOT A NARCOTICS
ADDICT?

SHALL WE PRETEND
YOU ARE NOT
WORRIED I WILL
CORRUPT THE
WHOLESOME
MEMBERS OF YOUR
SPORTY TEAM?

You do not say that.

I say that by saying, "Hey,
Coach, glad to be here." I
volunteer to do stuff like
stick around to pick up
balls, or bring the uniform
orders over to the office.

I say it by smiling and
leaving my locker open
and my backpack open so

it seems like I am hiding
nothing.

That is, I am doing a display
of hiding nothing,

Which means that in fact,

I am hiding something.

And what I am hiding is
that even though I am not
up to anything,

I have been a horror and an
addict.

A much bigger horror than
most people have ever been.

I hide it because the coaches
don't want to see it.

But I also know they know.

And I ALSO hide it
because the guys on the
team are curious if I will
ever show it.

I know they know about
me, but they don't
mention it.

I think some of them see
me as kind of gangster, and
it makes them wonder, or
think about me more than
they would otherwise.

Then there are others
who party. I can tell they
never bring it up around
me, never say they've been
drunk or high, never ever,
as if they are protecting me
from myself.

Adelaide?

                    I'm here.

Sorry that was a lot of
TEXTING FROM TOBY.

                    No, it was interesting.

Hey, Mom, today was
educational.

Hey, Coach, glad to be here.

Hey, guys, I'm sober.

I'm sober I'm sober I'm
sober I'm sober

I mean, I am sober, but

I have to actually perform
being sober to make other
people calm down. And
also, they don't really seem
that calm, so I am not sure
if my performance is a BAD
PERFORMANCE or if I am
wrong in thinking they need
this performance from me.

I am glad you are sober.

I know you are.

Are you glad you're sober?

I am glad.

Most of the time.

19

HOW TO LOVE SOMEONE

Uncle Benny's Fine Sandwiches, where Jack worked, was on a courtyard that bordered the Alabaster campus. Juniors and seniors often signed out at the main office and went there for lunch, in good weather.

Five days after he came upstairs and opened the box of condoms, four days after they played pinball, Adelaide hadn't heard from Jack. So she walked over to Uncle Benny's.

It did occur to her that their love might be a delicate flower that would wilt from too much attention.

On the other hand, maybe it was a delicate flower that would die if she neglected it.

Of course, Adelaide would rather think their connection was not a delicate flower at all, but a sturdy freaking cactus of a love, hardy and strong, able to withstand neglect and hard times—but then again, cacti are prickly. You need to approach them gently. Still, she went over. She wanted to see him.

The sandwich shop was empty except for two philosophers getting food to go. They took forever deciding. The windows were open and there wasn't any air-conditioning.

The only person working the counter was Oscar.

"Is Jack around?" Adelaide asked.

"It's you."

"Hi again. Is he working today?"

"Nope."

"Okay. Will you tell him I stopped by?"

"I might, if I see him," Oscar said. "Are you going to order anything?"

"I don't think so. I had lunch. Can I leave Jack a note?"

"If you must."

Adelaide had nothing to write on, so she took a napkin. She took some time, making doodles and swirls with her handwriting, but keeping the wording simple. "Came by to see you."

The shop was empty except for two philosophers getting food to go. Behind the counter was a sullen girl with a nose ring.

Jack was working in the kitchen, though. Adelaide saw him walk across the back room, where the grill was.

Her heart sped up. She walked out of the busy shop and around into the alley behind it, until she found the back door. It opened on a parking area lined with garbage cans.

Jack's Volkswagen Beetle was back there.

She looked into the car. There was a rust-colored jacket on the seat, and a library book about abstract painting.

She could hear Jack's voice through the screen door that led to the kitchen. "Pickles, Swiss cheese, two things of bacon, fresh tomatoes, sun-dried tomatoes, cheddar cheese, provolone." He was going through the fridge, calling out a list to someone else.

Maybe Adelaide should wait until he finished work. She'd be standing there, leaning on the hood of his car, when his shift ended. He'd break into a smile when he saw her.

———————————

As she stood there, a girl rode up on a bicycle. She was tall and flat-chested, with a round face, sweet full lips, and cheeks that were flushed with exercise. Straight Asian hair, long down her back, wearing jean shorts and a T-shirt. She didn't go to Alabaster.

Adelaide looked at her phone while the girl went up to Jack's VW and bent over the hood, scribbling a note on a pad of lined paper.

"Don't mind me," said the girl, smiling. "Love note."

Oh.

Jack had someone.

Who wasn't Adelaide.

He had this bicycle girl.

The girl leaned on the car as she wrote. She filled the front and back of her paper with loopy cursive, then folded the note and put it under Jack's windshield.

Jack was never going to tell Adelaide his secret pain.

He wasn't going to take her to the philosophy film series.

He might like her, might like her a lot, but he wasn't going to be *hers*. He wouldn't be utterly infatuated with

her and only her,

physically and mentally, the way

Adelaide had been with Mikey once, the way

Adelaide was now, with Jack.

What Adelaide wanted was to be

enmeshed with someone else.

She wanted to be unconditionally and exclusively adored.

She wanted to be the girl she used to be before Toby started getting high.

Jack wouldn't do that for her.

He had this bicycle girl to love. And the girl knew how to love someone; that seemed clear. There she was, pouring out her heart in this note, gleeful and generous and enjoying the moment.

Adelaide wasn't sure she knew how to love someone like that, at all.

The girl departed, waving briefly and throwing her leg over her bicycle, then pedaling down the alley as if pleased with her own romantic gesture.

Adelaide wanted to read the note, but she left it alone.

She had the urge to push through the door into the kitchen. Her whole body longed to be connected with his.

She should do it. Just show up. See the smile on his face.

She stepped inside.

Jack was lifting a bin of pickles.

"Hi," he said. "What are you doing here?"

"I came to see you."

"Oh yeah. Well. I'm at work."

"I was in the neighborhood."

"In the back alley?"

"I just—I thought I'd surprise you. Maybe you want to do something tonight, when you're done working?"

"I'm up to my elbows here. It's the lunch rush and we're short on cheese."

"I thought—"

"Look," Jack said, stopping to look her in the eye. "Wait outside. For a minute. Okay? Let me finish one thing and then I'll come out back. I'm glad you came by."

He smiled at her and her nerves went away. She remembered the way he'd drawn her to him, yanking her hand, and the way he'd kissed her, so urgently. The way they'd been, that night in her foldout bed.

She waited by his car. In a couple of minutes, Jack came down the small set of steps from the back door, wiping sweat off his forehead with his forearm.

"Adelaide, look, I should have been clear. I'm not—I'm not available."

"Oh."

"I shouldn't have kissed you. Or gone home with you. Or if I did, I should have been clear about exactly what my feelings are."

She felt her face heat up. She didn't know what to do with her hands. "Yeah, okay."

"Can I tell you something? I feel like you deserve an honest explanation."

"Sure."

"You make me uncomfortable."

"What? How?"

"You want saving or something. A rescuer."

"No, I don't."

"You do, and I don't want to rescue anyone."

"I don't know what you mean."

"For example, walking in the rain, three miles from home, in the pitch dark. Why not just take a cab? It was like you wanted to be unhappy."

"I didn't have money for a cab."

"You couldn't get a ride from anyone you know? Or splurge on it? It's asking for trouble to be walking in the dark on that road."

"You don't know how much money I have," Adelaide snapped. "And you don't get to tell me how to get home."

"It seems like a thing with you, is all. Like you want me to rescue you from loneliness. Or boredom. Or from whatever happened with your old boyfriend."

"I was just into you. Is that a crime?"

He shook his head. "It's not my job to rescue you, Adelaide."

"I rescued *you* at the dog run," Adelaide argued. "I got B-Cake back for you."

She wanted to rescue Jack, actually. She wanted to save him from the sadness of his mother's death; to show him a

176

clear, patient, empathetic love; to heal the pain she imagined in his hips.

Jack blew out a breath. "Thank you for your help with the dog. You're exceptionally pretty and obviously very smart, Adelaide. But— you look at me like I'm an object, and you talk to me like you don't see me at all. You have ideas about me that you made up. Do you hear me? You made them up. I've met a lot of girls who pity me and want to save me. Or they think I fit some idea they have of a tragic hero."

"Stop," she said. "You don't get to make me the bad guy here. You don't." Sweat ran down her neck. "What you really mean is,

I'm not that into you.

But that's not what

you say.

You say

there's something I did wrong, because that takes the heat off you.

The problem with people like you is, they're

not capable of love. They're

shut off. They're

scared. They're

dealing with other stuff in their lives, whatever—but they know inside, it's

their hearts that are closed." She shook her head to clear it. "What I mean is, you're saying

I want rescuing, and you say

I'm imagining stuff about you, and you say
I look at you like an object, and—"

"That's how it feels on my end," Jack cut in. "You don't know me at all. You just like the *idea* of me, the way I fit into some fantasy you have of a boyfriend. And it's mixed with pity and a kind of morbid curiosity about pain and physical difference and curiosity about my mother dying and— Ugh. I hate it."

"That's called liking a guy when you don't know him that well," said Adelaide. "You like the
idea of a person, so you
want to get to know him. It's called
not being closed off, and
going after what you want, and
it's completely awful for you to go telling me
there's something *wrong* with me and
that's why you don't want me, when really,
you don't want me because your own heart is
cold. It's just a
nothing little heart."

"That's not true, Adelaide," said Jack.

"I think it is."

"It's *not*."

"Then what is it?"

"I'm just not that into you," he said.

Jack blew out a breath. "Thank you for your help with the dog. You're exceptionally pretty and obviously very smart,

Adelaide. But— you look at me like I'm an object, and you talk to me like you don't see me at all. You have ideas about me that you made up. Do you hear me? You made them up. I've met a lot of girls who pity me and want to save me. Or they think I fit some idea they have of a tragic hero. I'm just— Ugh. I work in a sandwich shop and I'm trying to start over in a school I haven't been at for two years, and I just lost my mother. I'm not in any shape to have a girlfriend. So I shouldn't have kissed you."

"Multiple times," she put in. "And all the other stuff."

"I know. I'm not smart about these things sometimes."

"You seemed like you wanted to. You took me swimming and brought me bacon."

"I did want to, at the time. But I'm done. I can't deal with your unhappiness on top of mine."

Your unhappiness on top of mine. How did he see her so clearly? How did he know she was unhappy, when even Mikey hadn't known, at least not consciously?

He turned and went back up the stairs to the sandwich shop kitchen.

"Jack, wait," she called.

She thought maybe he would turn around and change his mind. Some force
bigger than them both would lead him to
run back to her,
fall into her,
wrap his arms around her and give her his
wounded but beautiful heart
and body.
But Jack just opened the screen door and went back to work.

Texts.

Jack, you have a girlfriend.

. . .

. . .

. . .

You should have told me you have a girlfriend.

She's not exactly my girlfriend.

You should have told me you were seeing someone.

I just moved here. You and I only hung out a couple times.

We're not exclusive, Adelaide.

I saw her leave a note on your car.

180

Sorry.

                    . . .

                    . . .

                    Okay, yeah, you and I only
                    hung out a couple times.

                    But you came home with me,
                    Jack. And so I thought—I
                    thought maybe we—

                    I was surprised, is all. That
                    you'd come home with me
                    when you like someone else.

                    I should just shut up now.

I think she is my girlfriend,
actually.

                    . . .

                    . . .

                    Got it.

But Adelaide! In some
other universe,

some other time and
place, it might have gone
differently. It might have
been you and me.

So I really am sorry. Really,
really.

20

AM I THE PERSON?

Texts.

Save me. I cannot tolerate our
mother.

How so?

She is on tiptoe. ALL THE
TIME.

Around you?

Around me. She is scared
of me.

No.

Yes, she is.

I mean, she's scared of the
addict inside me. It is super
annoying.

> Are you scared of the addict
> inside you?

. . .

. . .

Yes.

Here's the thing I have
been thinking about.

> I'm listening.

In meetings, you have to
say, I am a narcotics addict.

> And?

And . . .

I have said it a hundred
times. Because you have to
say it. But . . .

It's true and it's also not
true.

It feels more like there's an
addict inside me but the
addict isn't me.

I mean

I am not the guy who did
that stuff.

I know I am.

But also I'm not.

What stuff?

I AM NOT THE GUY
WHO did narcotics and
told the lies and took
cash from your wallet and
wouldn't talk to you and
acted terrible in therapy
and was just a thunder-butt.

I mean, I did all that stuff.
I just don't want to walk
around every day saying
to myself, I am a complete

and utter shit. I feel like a
reasonably nice human.

I would rather say I used to
be an addict.

But that is NOT what you
are supposed to say.

You have to say, I am an
addict.

If I could say I used to be
an addict, there would be
no reason for Mom to be
scared.

But maybe she should be
scared.

Some days are hard. I just
want to go numb.

                    What do you do then?

I have a sponsor. I call him.

                    Hug.

I take a shower, play video
games. Meditate. DON'T
LAUGH.

I'm not laughing. I'm not.

I can relate to wanting to be
numb. I mean, it's not the
same but maybe it's similar.
My boyfriend Mikey dumped
me at the start of the summer
and I have just NOT BEEN
RIGHT since then.

Mom said it was a mutual
decision. And very mature
because you were too
young to be spending all
summer together anyway.

No.

He dropped me.

He ran away, basically.

I'm sorry.

And now I— Well. There has
been a lot of DRAMA. Most
of it inside my head. And even
though the drama is over, it's
still going on in my head, if
that makes sense. I can't let it
go or make it stop.

So I would like to go numb.
All your sober-living numbing
ideas much appreciated.

Plants vs. Zombies works
pretty good.

Ha.

Seriously, it does.

You were saying about Mom?

Yeah. So the way it feels is

That there is an addict
inside me but

I am not the addict.

And Mom is scared of the
addict.

Justifiably scared,

Like it might take me over,
like a werewolf changing at
the full moon.

And she can't trust the me
that's here because of the
addict that's inside

. . .

. . .

Adelaide?

                              Sorry.

?

                              I am crying.

Don't cry.

                              It's not your fault. I'm just

Don't cry. I am ok. I am
sober.

My lunch hour is over. I
gotta go. But . . .

Your werewolf little
brother is thinking of you
even when he is at work.

Bye.

Hug.

Wait. What happened with
Darcy?

You give good advice. 😊

But my sponsor
reminded me:

I'm not supposed to have
any "relationships" for at
least a year. It's a sober
thing. So, ugh. I fessed up.
Told her I was a recovering
addict. And that I like her
but I can't.

And?

She was skeeved out. She
went home immediately.
And wouldn't look me in
the eye for three days. But
now she talks to me again.
Just a little. And we got
food with a group of other

junior counselors after work
the other day. So it's not
the worst.

                    Oh blergh. Boo.

Yeah. Boo.

PART III

21

MIKEY DOUBLE L
IN MULTIPLE UNIVERSES

Adelaide ate dinner with her father in the evenings and when they'd finished cleaning up, he'd call Rebecca and retire to his bedroom to chat.

He'd say, "Oh, I'm glad to hear your voice," or, "I was thinking of you today." Adelaide said hi and talked to her mom when she needed to, but she hardly understood Levi's enthusiasm. Her mother was either in a haze of unmedicated sciatica pain, through which she asked stilted questions about Adelaide's well-being, or she was lively but mired in a puddle of worries. Some of the worries were semi-reasonable (Was it okay for Toby to go with friends to a party, or should she say no?) and some were agonizingly trivial (Was Adelaide still drinking diet soda? Because she'd read an article that details all the ways it's poison). That was how Rebecca showed she cared: with agitation and questions about good nutrition, sleep, life balance, fresh air. Plus whale emojis.

In the mornings, Adelaide walked the dogs. Afterward, she lay on the couches in the owners' living rooms, tired and hot. She napped that way in the late mornings, letting the dogs snarfle around and finally settle down in homes that were not their own. Over the days, she drank a case of seltzer in the house belonging to Pretzel's owner, a divorced science teacher with two young kids.

She felt bad about drinking the seltzer and told herself she'd replace it.

She worked on her model of *Fool for Love.*

She cut cardboard with X-Acto knives.

She etched tiny

bricks into the walls and into the visible foundation of the motel.

She built a tiny ceiling fan and made miniature electrical sockets.

Stacey S came back for another overnight.

"You're still in love with Mikey, that's my evaluation," she said, when she heard about the end of things with Jack. The two of them were shopping for non-ugly bras on a limited budget at a store called Henrietta's Dancewear and Lingerie on the opposite end of town from Alabaster.

"I am not in love with Mikey."

"You need to get out of love."

"I did get out of love."

"I don't think so. I think it's still all about Mikey."

"Don't get psychological on me."

"Okay, fine," said Stacey, going into the tiny dressing room to try things on and speaking through the flowered curtain. "I just want you to be happy. Did I tell you Camilla went for coffee with her ex-girlfriend and supposedly forgot to tell me? I literally heard it from her mom, who was like, 'Oh, she's out to coffee with Jane.' I called the house because she didn't pick up her cell. And then Camilla was all, 'Oh, I thought I told you about it, I would never not tell you,' and also 'It was just coffee, and I shouldn't have to tell you everything.'"

"She's a little bit bad news," said Adelaide.

"No she's not. She's good news. This bra is terrible."

"Secret ex-girlfriend activities are bad news to me."

"No. It's just this coffee thing, this one time. She seemed really insincere, is all. I was like, 'Well, I'm going to go see Adelaide, then, and you can have coffee with Jane all freaking weekend if you want to, because whatever, I won't even be here.'"

"Aw, you miss her!" said Adelaide.

"Damn it, that's the truth," said Stacey.

"Do you want to call her?"

"Kind of. Oh, this bra is good, you can look." Adelaide peeked in. Stacey's bra was electric green. "I'm getting it in this and the pink," said Stacey.

"I think there's yellow, too."

"Okay. Are you going to try stuff on?"

"Yeah, I'll try the weird brown one and this flower one while you go call Camilla."

"You think I should?"

"Yes," said Adelaide. "Give me the bras and you can step outside."

197

Stacey S was still preoccupied with college applications. Adelaide found her shockingly ambitious. They had both taken the tests and written early drafts of the common application essay. Alabaster forced them to do all that. But Stacey, with her spreadsheets and bookmarked web pages, took on the college process with ferocity. She had brought a big book of colleges with her on the bus. The pages were marked with sticky notes in different colors.

"When it's finished, you have to photograph the set model you're building for your portfolio," she told Adelaide later as they ate almond croissants in their favorite café.

Adelaide sighed. "My dad said the same thing. Especially given that my grades are bad. He said I need a portfolio of art to show my strengths. But it kind of makes me vomit."

"No, don't vomit," said Stacey. "The model sounds amazing. You should photograph your Lego dioramas too."

"Colleges don't want to see Lego."

"Maybe they do. I like the one you did for me." Adelaide had made Stacey a Lego version of their dorm room.

"My Lego things are mostly back in Baltimore, actually."

"Aren't you going home this summer?"

"Not if I can help it."

The college process made Adelaide feel overwhelmed and ashamed. She couldn't really conceive of life beyond next year at Alabaster. She was just trying to get through the summer. She wasn't a planner, even at her best, but at present she was consumed by her own thoughts, unable to focus her attention on the world beyond her.

Some mornings, listening to NPR podcasts with her father, Adelaide resolved to pay attention to the news. The country was going to hell, after all. There were rights to fight for; there were causes to learn about. She would plan to read a certain number of articles every day, but the resolve never lasted more than a single morning. The magnetic pull of her interior life was too strong.

Damn. It was nearly eleven o'clock. Adelaide bolted awake.

She was late to take the dogs out. Very late.

Stacey was still asleep next to her.

She threw herself into her clothes, grabbed her enormous ring of keys, and ran.

GG Pan was the most likely to poop on the floor, so Adelaide went to his place first.

Yes, he had done it.

She took him and Voldemort out, leaving the poop where it was because Voldie was so uncomfortable.

She planned to go back in and clean, but as soon as she got outdoors she realized she should go to EllaBella's place right away.

EllaBella ran outside without waiting for Adelaide to clip her leash on.

Poor dog. It had been nineteen hours.

Adelaide brought the three of them to Pretzel's place. Pretzel had made a big, foul-smelling puddle on the antique rug.

At Rabbit's house, Rabbit trotted inside, looking over her shoulder. Adelaide followed with all the dogs, and Rabbit showed them a puddle with a pig poop next to it. *I'm really sorry*, said Rabbit.

Since this was the last dog, Adelaide decided to clean this one up now. She unclipped the leashes and looked for paper towels and cleaning supplies.

Big mistake. The loose dogs, curious about Rabbit's mess, ran over to sniff it. They stepped in it, then trotted away, tracking poop and urine across rugs and floors, even up onto the couch.

Adelaide broke. She sat down on the floor and began to cry.

She thought, *I deserve this.*

It's my fault for staying up late.

For forgetting to set the alarm on my phone.

These poor lonely dogs trusted me and I let them down for no good reason.

Adelaide's phone pinged.

It was a text from Mikey.

Hey there. How are you?

He had reached out now and again over the past couple of weeks, while he was in Puerto Rico. He still wanted to be friends.

Adelaide was glad he missed her.

She always composed her texts back to him six different ways before sending, trying to show him how happy she was without him. But right now, with the dog pee disaster unfolding around her, she wrote:

> I have been texting with my brother a lot. I never told you this, but he's in recovery.

She hoped Mikey's heart would go out to her, now that she'd revealed the cause of the sadness she never mentioned to him that had nonetheless stopped him from loving her.

Now she would tell him about it.

Some part of his Mikey soul would reach out and remember how he loved her.

He texted back:

> Whoa. That's good he is recovering, though!

Except, you know, he didn't love her.

She always composed her texts back to him six different ways before sending, trying to show him how happy she was without him. But right now, with the dog pee disaster unfolding around her, she wrote:

> I have reached a level of despair where I am sitting in dog urine.

Mikey typed,

> Ha!

> Seriously.

> Very funny. Xo

Adelaide felt dismissed. She had showed her real, disgusting situation to Mikey and he had dismissed her. Had he ever *really* wanted to hear the truth about her life?

Her phone pinged.

There was a text from Mikey Double L. It was a photo of them at the spring formal. Adelaide was wearing a strapless black dress and laughing so hard her gums showed. Mikey had his arms wrapped around her. They had been dancing, and he looked sweaty in his clean white shirt and green tie. But clean sweaty, like always.

A second later came another picture. From just a couple of minutes later on the same night, a selfie of the two of them kissing. Adelaide's chin looked weird. Mikey looked hot.

And a third text:

> Us.

Adelaide looked at the photos for a long time. She stood up and walked to Rabbit's kitchen. She cleaned up the mess and all the doggie footprints. She scrubbed the stain off the couch. She got the dogs leashed and washed her hands.

Then she texted Mikey back:

There is no us anymore.

Her phone pinged.

There was a text from Mikey Double L. It was a photo.

And then another.

And a third text:

Us.

Adelaide texted him back.

Hi.

The phone rang. "I miss you," he said when she answered.

"I miss you too."

"I owe you seventeen apologies. I wish I could see you right now and say everything that needs saying in person. It's so awkward on the phone."

He could see her, of course. He was back from Puerto Rico and he lived only three hours away.

"I'm with the dogs," she said. "There was a poop catastrophe this morning of truly epic proportions."

"How's that going?"

"The catastrophe? It's nearly cleared up," she lied. "And the dogs love me," she said. "So that's a plus."

"I love you."

"What?"

"I made a terrible mistake, breaking up with you."

She didn't say anything.

"I don't know what I was thinking," said Mikey, his wonderful, familiar voice in her ear. "It was just stupid. I got scared of being together all summer. Without our friends. It seemed too intense. I got home, and at first, I was relieved. But then, in Puerto Rico, all I thought about was you. I couldn't even look at other girls."

Adelaide was suddenly

gloriously happy. It was

terrible to be

gloriously happy that

Mikey was

sad, and

terrible even to be

gloriously happy that

Mikey loved her,

since Adelaide had been a complete failure at happiness when he didn't love her. It was, after all, a bad idea to hinge your happiness on someone *else's* feelings.

But that was just how it was. She did hinge them.

"I miss you, Adelaide," Mikey said. "I miss you so much. Will you let me come see you?"

"Yes," she said. "You can come see me."

22

OSCAR, TERRANCE, PERLA, AND THE M&M'S

Adelaide felt clearheaded for the first time all summer.

Stacey was right. Everything about Jack was really about Mikey Double L.

And Jack was right. She *had*

objectified and idealized him and been weird about his physical difference and his scars and his grief.

Hadn't seen him truly.

But that was because she was

incapable of seeing him truly, because

the person she loved was Mikey Double L.

She couldn't wait to hear his voice in her ear and to smell his clean Mikey smell again; to feel his shoulder muscles under her hands and to look into his open face and feel happy again.

Her father said Mikey could stay with them, but he had to sleep on the living room couch. Adelaide said fine and Mikey said he had to work at the fencing camp all week but he'd arrive at the bus stop at ten p.m. on Friday.

Adelaide planned to meet him there, in front of the main campus entrance, by the fountain that displayed the unofficial school symbol, a fish statue everyone called the Guppy.

Close to ten, she walked over. She planned for Mikey to come meet the dogs right away, since she had to walk them before bed.

But Mikey wasn't there yet. Instead, Perla Izad was sitting on the broad ledge of the fountain's pool, talking to Oscar and Terrance.

"Good evening," said Perla.

"Adelaide!" said Oscar. "We've been to the movies."

"Hi," Adelaide said, scanning around for Mikey. "You guys know each other?"

"We do now," said Perla. "We met this evening at the philosophy film series."

"It was the creepiest film," said Terrance.

"Catherine Deneuve was good, though," said Oscar. "Terrance and I snuck in, even though we don't go here."

"You didn't sneak in," said Perla. "The film series is open to the public."

"I felt like we were sneaking in," said Oscar.

"Everyone there was in college," said Terrance. "It definitely felt weird."

"The movie was sexist," said Perla, "but also symphonic."

"Symphonic, seriously?" said Oscar.

"I like big words." Perla collapsed in giggles. Adelaide wondered if they had been smoking pot.

"I don't think you really know what *symphonic* means." Oscar turned to Adelaide. "The director was Roman Polanski. He's a very creepy person. Except the movie was also amazing. We're debating whether we can like it."

"I don't think we can, actually," said Terrance.

"Deneuve had good hair," said Perla. "How did she get it like that? Do you think it was a wig?"

Oscar shrugged. "I have no understanding of hair."

"My friend is supposed to meet me here," Adelaide said. "Did you see an Asian guy, short hair, waiting?"

"We did not," said Terrance.

"Do you know if the bus came already?"

"We would have remembered," said Perla. "We've been sitting here for, what, I think two hours? Yael was with us for a while, but she went to bed at least an hour ago."

"Her name was Yael?" said Oscar. "I forgot her name."

"Yes. She goes to Oberlin."

"Ooh, I want to go to Oberlin. They have a music conservatory."

Adelaide looked at her phone She didn't have any texts. She sent Mikey one:

I'm here. Where are you?

"My advice," said Perla, "is if he makes you wait, he's not worth waiting for."

Terrance laughed.

"I'm worried something happened to him," Adelaide said.

A text from Mikey pinged back.

207

I sent you an email earlier.
Didn't you get it?

Adelaide almost never checked her email in the summer.
She checked now.
He had emailed her this morning.

Dear Adelaide,

I've been up all night thinking.

I shouldn't come visit.

I do miss you and I do have feelings for you, but I'm
too confused right now. I have to sort myself out.

Mikey

Adelaide texted back:

Why would you send that
by email?

And Mikey didn't answer.
And still he didn't answer.
She texted again:

Why? I didn't see it till
now.

Oscar, Terrance, and Perla had been talking.

"Did you get stood up?" Perla asked Adelaide.

Adelaide nodded. She bit her lip.

"Come sit with us," said Oscar.

"Whoever it was doesn't deserve you," said Perla. "And the night is beautiful."

"We have peanut M&M's," said Terrance. "Or Perla does." Perla rummaged in her tote bag and pulled out a giant bag of them, half-full.

Adelaide took a couple. She concentrated on the two-part crunch between her teeth, candy coating and then peanut. She concentrated so she wouldn't cry. "I used to wish on the green ones," she said. "With my brother."

"Here, let's all get green ones, then," said Oscar. Perla let him peer into the M&M's. He found a green and held it up. "What do we do?"

"Don't talk to each other when we're chewing or our wish won't come true," said Adelaide.

"Wait," said Perla. "We should all do it at once."

"Okay," agreed Oscar.

"Wait, I need one," said Terrance, standing up to look in the bag.

All four of them took a moment to wish.

Adelaide wished to love someone and be loved back.

And to love someone and know that it was him she loved, not some idea of him.

Maybe that was two wishes. Maybe it was only one.

They chewed their M&M's in silence.

Then Adelaide left them and went to take care of the dogs.

+ + +

She brought EllaBella home last, that evening. She wandered through Mr. Byrd's house, turning on the lights. She looked at his books. There were so many they wouldn't fit on his shelves. They were piled on the coffee table.

The office was the biggest room in the house. EllaBella had a dog bed there, and there were free weights in the corner. There was a large framed print of a young Black man, surrounded by flowers, like an old-style portrait made modern.

Adelaide knew she shouldn't wander around Byrd's house this way. She just wanted to . . . well, see who he was. How he lived.

His bed had blue sheets and pillowcases.

The master bathroom had several different kinds of moisturizers.

She lay on his bed, on top of the blankets. The pillows were cool in their blue pillowcases.

EllaBella got up there with her. Adelaide flicked on Mr. Byrd's television, flipping through the channels.

Adults like him probably knew how to love other people so that the other people liked it.

They didn't talk too much. They weren't too angry or too sad.

They were loved back, by their lovers, by their siblings.

They didn't get overly attached to dogs who didn't even belong to them.

23

ADELAIDE'S BROTHER,
A STORY IN TWELVE STEPS

Texts.

Adelaide.

Toby.

In 12-step we apologize to
people we wronged while
we were high.

I know. You apologized to me
already.

I want to apologize again.

I was a selfish stupid horror
person to you. I hope I
haven't ruined us forever,
because you are my sister
and I think you're cool.

This morning I found some
of the letters you wrote me
when I was in rehab. And
the instax photos you sent.

I never wrote you back.

It's okay.

It was like I wasn't even me
then.

I wasn't the werewolf,
either. I was like, I don't
know, a cold rock.

Rocks cannot write
postcards. Or text. They
totally suck at being
brothers.

So that's what I'm sorry for.

When you were in Kingsmont,
you know Mom and Dad
mostly told me not to visit,
right? They said, Don't visit.
That's why I sent you mail.

But I wish I had visited.

The letters are good,
actually. I'm gonna keep
them till they're super old
and get them out again on
your fiftieth birthday.

Weirdo.

24

FOOL FOR LOVE
IN SEVERAL
POSSIBLE WORLDS

Adelaide knew she was close to finishing the model for Kaspian-Lee, but her lighting rig had been refusing to attach. In fact, she had broken the rig at one point and been forced to start it over. Now she had a new idea for getting it to stretch across the top of the box.

When she fastened the rig as planned, nothing went wrong. The pieces slid into the grooves she had made for them. The hot-glue gun worked.

She was looking at a complete model.

It was a motel room glazed in reflective paint,
   like the paint they use to put white stripes down the middle of the road.
   The seedy furniture sat oddly in this

surreal, almost
transcendent room that
glowed and flickered from
floor to ceiling.

———————————————

It was a room strewn with
feathers from pillows ripped open.
Feathers coated the walls and the
chairs and the table. All May's
possessions were
red, like her dress. Her
suitcase was red,
her coffee mug,
the hangers she used for her clothes.

———————————————

It was a motel room filled with
skeletons of people who had
slept there before. There were
skeletons in the chairs,
skeletons under the bed, even a
skeleton in the
bathtub you could glimpse through a door.

———————————————

It was a solid gold motel room, with walls of exposed gold
brick. The bed hung on the wall, unmade. It was larger than

a normal double bed too, and it faced the audience, dead center.

There was a

television. And a

coffee maker. Both looked

pitifully cheap, varnished gold.

May also had a number of

postcards stuck to a sad little corkboard. They weren't gold, but served as evidence of

May's interior life beyond the room.

Outside the window was nothing but

dirt, with a few old tin cans buried in it.

Below the motel room you could see the

foundation and the

dirt on which that lay, and under it,

two human skeletons buried together, their bones entwined.

It expressed, Adelaide felt, the

weird grandiosity of the human mind.

May and Eddie, the lovers in the play, definitely had that weird grandiosity.

And the play itself did too.

Adelaide had made this strange object during this lonely, obsessive, egg-yolk-of-misery summer, and she was

proud of it.

The teacher was in the studio when Adelaide arrived with the finished model. B-Cake was snarfling around the floor, looking for something to eat.

"Congratulations," said Kaspian-Lee.

"On what?"

"I'm stunned," said Kaspian-Lee. "I always suspected you had an original mind. You understand the way a creative project can hang together even though the parts don't seem related to one another. You comprehend the way something ridiculous or surreal can reveal something deeply true about human experience. This work is wildly fresh and strange, Adelaide Buchwald."

"Thank you."

"I have seen many, many designs for *Fool for Love*, but never has one moved me like this one does. I can see the tragedy of May and Eddie written on the walls. It's beneath the floors before the show even starts, and the tragedy is compelling and simultaneously dirty and ugly, like a stain. These characters can't escape it."

Adelaide felt a rush of validation. She was good at this. She had been seen.

The teacher was in the studio when Adelaide arrived with the finished model. B-Cake was snarfling around the floor, looking for something to eat.

"We have to have a discussion."

"Okay."

"Because you didn't do the assignment."

"What?"

"It's not the assignment," Kaspian-Lee repeated. "Are you surprised?"

"Very."

"I can't see why."

"I was careful with the measurements," Adelaide told her. "And it's a motel room. It has all the things you need for the story—I mean, I figured the coffee maker would also make tea. Eddie offers tea, not coffee. I know that."

"It doesn't serve the play." Kaspian-Lee said it neutrally, as if it were a fact, not an opinion.

"What do you mean?"

"You put so much Adelaide Buchwald into it, there's no Sam Shepard."

"And that's bad?"

"Set design is meant to assist in telling the story the playwright has put into words. What you have done is play with gold spray paint and put a lot of obvious symbols all over the place," said the teacher. "I wasn't asking you for an amateur art project. I was asking you to facilitate Shepard's storytelling."

"Can't you listen to my defense? I prepared answers to all the prompts you gave me. I worked really hard."

"When you tell me how hard you worked, you miss the point," said Kaspian-Lee. "The work you put in is irrelevant. The result is what matters. And this design fundamentally fails, because it's nothing but you showing off. I'm sorry, Adelaide, but it's true."

It was futile. Adelaide couldn't please Kaspian-Lee. She couldn't please *anyone*, actually. Not her mother (who was so needy),

her brother (who was so often blank),

Mikey Double L (who wanted someone happy),

Jack Cavallero (who wasn't interested),

the dean's office (which put her on academic probation), nor

the college admissions officers potentially looking at her

crappy transcript.

Rage flooded her veins. She picked up her model and

threw it to the floor of the studio. She

stomped on it and

hit it with a

metal three-hole punch. She

ripped it and

kicked it until the

stupid ugly thing was in shreds.

Adelaide left the

wreckage

on the floor of the classroom as Kaspian-Lee stared at her,

openmouthed.

"Wait," said Adelaide.

Kaspian-Lee turned.

"You don't get to treat people like that. I don't care who you are or what you're going through, you don't get to trash people's projects like they mean nothing."

"You're trying to prevent something that's already happened," said Kaspian-Lee calmly.

"I know you're not interested in hearing me talk," Adelaide

said. "I know you're not interested in why I did the design like I did, but you should seriously evaluate your personal skills, because they're terrible."

A long moment passed.

Finally, Kaspian-Lee said, "You make a point, actually. You know, I'm very recently through with Martin Schlegel and his pornographic imagination."

"What?"

"I have left Mr. Schlegel. B-Cake and I won't be going to the seashore after all. I'm having something of a personal crisis."

"Oh."

"I haven't been sleeping. Or eating, for that matter," said Kaspian-Lee. "It's like there's . . ." She trailed off.

"An ugly, slimy, viscous membrane between the rest of the world and you?" said Adelaide. "And the membrane is the breakup? An egg yolk of misery?"

"Precisely," said Kaspian-Lee.

Adelaide brought the model home. She set it on the dining table.

She called Toby. She hadn't heard his voice all summer.

"Hi, Adelaide."

"Toby."

"What's up? I'm on lunch break."

"My lunatic teacher decided she

hated my Set Design project, and I don't even know what she

hated so much except that it had

too many details or was

too shiny or I

showed off too much or something, even though it was super neat and all the measurements were perfect, and then

I scolded her and told her she had terrible social skills.

I think she flunked me, which means I've

failed academic probation, which means I'm

very likely coming back to Baltimore, but I don't even know for sure because I was too busy scolding her to even find out. And

Mikey said he loved me and

wanted me back, but then he

changed his mind. This guy

Jack I was seeing

wants nothing to do with me.

And I feel like I can see a

future with Jack, and I can see a

past with him,

versions of the past that didn't happen. I can see them, like memories.

It feels important somehow. Like it matters more than any other relationship ever could. But then, maybe it's just my feelings for Mikey blurring and smooshing together with my feelings for Jack, so that when

I think I love Jack, really it's that

I love Mikey, and the truth is

I have some

romantic obsessional tendencies. Like, I just told you it

matters more than any other relationship ever could, but I'm not even seeing him. There's nothing between us anymore.

Maybe I even have, like, an

addiction to love, or to relationships or something.

It's like being in love makes me feel better, much better, than I do the rest of the time. Except when

it makes me miserable.

Maybe it's an

endorphin rush? Or a

validation?

Romantic obsessional tendency—that is not a good quality in a person.

I made this beautiful model, Toby, and it took me the whole summer, but then Kaspian-Lee told me it wasn't beautiful after all.

She almost

changed

how

I

feel

about the thing that I made, and that just feels wrong, do you know?

Shouldn't

I

decide

how

I

feel

about the thing I made?"

"Adelaide," Toby interrupted, his voice sweet. "Are you high?"

"No. No. I'm not high. I'm not high."

"You're sounding scary. And weird."

Adelaide took a shaky breath. "I'm not okay. I'm not okay right now. But I'm not high."

"Okay."

"Okay."

"Do you want to start from the beginning?" Toby asked. "I have half an hour before I have to go back to work."

So she did.

PART IV

25

A MAULING, IN A WORLD NOT YET ENCOUNTERED

It was the third day of Adelaide Buchwald's summer job, the summer after her junior year at boarding school. Her job was to walk five dogs, morning and night. They all belonged to teachers who were on summer vacation.

The morning she met Jack, Adelaide took them all to the dog run on the Alabaster Preparatory Academy campus. The run was a sandy space, fenced in and surrounded by trees. She unleashed the dogs and sat on a bench while they frolicked.

She texted her mom about the breakup with Mikey.

Lord Voldemort and Pretzel played chase. Rabbit growled at something on the other side of the fence.

And suddenly, a boy appeared. He was already in the run when Adelaide saw him, standing under a tree. He had a fluffy white dog on a leash.

Adelaide recognized the dog. It was B-Cake. B-Cake belonged to Sunny Kaspian-Lee.

A beat later, Adelaide recognized the boy as well, though she was sure she'd never seen him at Alabaster. When he turned, he had a sweet V-shaped face and full lips. He was broad in the shoulders, with a narrow nose, smooth-shaven face, delicate ears. His light brown hair was wavy and a little wild. He was the sort of person you'd see immortalized in Roman statuary, his skin a warm Mediterranean olive, his chin and neck strong.

She knew him. She was certain of it.

She remembered his walk.

The boy released the clip on the leash. B-Cake zoomed over to Rabbit and Rabbit exploded into the air with an anxious yip.

The boy laughed, covering his mouth with his fist. "Poor puppy," he said.

The dog Rabbit jumped the fence.

B-Cake followed.

Adelaide and Jack gave chase, though Jack wasn't much use, holding the leash and calling "Birthday! Come here, Birthday!"

B-Cake and Rabbit were tumbling on the lawn next to Hobbs Hall, running in manic circles. Adelaide tackled Rabbit, a pit bull of no delicate build, grabbing her around the chest with one hand.

Rabbit barked aggressively and B-Cake circled, yapping.

Adelaide struggled to keep hold of Rabbit, and before she knew it, the dog's teeth had clamped onto her wrist. Hard.

"Let go, Rabbit!" she yelled. "Drop it!" (Not that Rabbit *ever* dropped anything when told.)

The bite was no joke. Rabbit latched on and began shaking her head back and forth, her teeth puncturing Adelaide's skin. Tearing it. Blood spattered as the dog shook her arm. Adelaide pulled on Rabbit's ear with her other hand. "Let me go!"

But Rabbit held on.

Jack appeared, standing over them. He bent over and punched Rabbit in the face, hitting her right in the nose.

Rabbit staggered but kept her teeth where they were, so Jack punched her again.

Rabbit released Adelaide's arm and dropped her body low to the ground, slinking off in shame. Tail between her legs. Whimpering.

Adelaide clutched her arm to her chest. "Thank you."

"Are you okay?" Jack asked.

She was not. She couldn't feel any pain, but she was bleeding enormously. She knew she should look at it, but she couldn't bear to take her hand off the wound she had instinctively covered.

Jack took off his shirt.

God, he was good-looking.

Adelaide felt dizzy, like there wasn't enough blood in her head. It was all gushing out of her wrist. Why was his shirt off? Could she be hallucinating?

She could see he had B-Cake on the leash again.

Had he actually bothered to catch B-Cake before punching Rabbit? So Kaspian-Lee would be sure to get her dog back? Or had he done it afterward?

What kind of person leashes a dog when someone's wrist is being mauled?

Oh, his shirt was still off. Wow.

He handed her the shirt.

She wrapped it around her wrist to slow the bleeding.

Now she could feel the wound. A sharp, burning sensation that radiated up her arm.

Rabbit was huddled by the fence, chin on the ground. *I'm sorry*, she said. *I'm such a bad dog. I know not to do that. I know better. I'm such a bad dog.*

"You have to go to the hospital," said Jack.

You have always been nice to me, said Rabbit. *I got overexcited. That boy makes me nervous. Please don't hate me.*

"I have to get the dogs home. I can't leave them here," Adelaide said. The thought of trying to give Jack her keys, explaining to him all the addresses—she didn't even *know* the addresses, just where the houses were—it seemed impossible.

Jack still didn't have his shirt on. Well, of course he didn't. He had a scar on one side of his abdomen, a large, raised one. Light-headed, Adelaide wondered what had happened to him.

Her blood started to seep through the cotton.

"Okay, here's what we're going to do," she told him. "I'm going to get all the dogs on leash. Rabbit will be okay. She's really sorry. She doesn't like you, though. I'm going to bring the dogs back to their houses. And you're going to come with me just in case I faint or something. When we get the last dog in, we're calling my dad. But not before, or he'll try to take me to the hospital before the dogs are brought home."

The boy nodded.

"Okay," said Adelaide. "Let's do it."

At the hospital, Levi called Adelaide's mother and put her on speaker. "Oh, my pudding, are you okay?"

"I'm superlative," said Adelaide. "Considering."

"That's what you always say," said Rebecca. "But I think you put on a brave face sometimes."

It was true. But Adelaide didn't want to risk her mother spiraling into anxiety. "I'm fine. You don't need to worry."

"I'm coming up," said Rebecca. "Toby and I are going to drive. I'm literally packing right now. We'll be there in . . . well, six and a half hours sounds reasonable. We may hit traffic."

"I don't think you have to come," said Adelaide. "I got stitches already. And antibiotics. I get to go home soon."

"It's just paperwork now, at the hospital," said Levi. "The dog has had all her shots. We talked to the owner."

"I'm putting pajamas in the suitcase," said Rebecca. "And bras. And socks. I'm getting Toby from group and we're driving up. Oh, I have to pack his stuff too."

"You don't need to come," repeated Adelaide.

"I want to see you, pudding. Just let me come be a mom.

"Okay, fine."

"Good. Do you think Toby needs extra shoes, or will he be fine with the shoes he has on?"

"Extra shoes."

"Okay. Ugh. His room is so messy."

"Hey, what does your whale emoji mean?"

"Like I send in texts? My whale?"

"Yeah."

Rebecca paused. "It's just a jolly whale. I don't like the smiley-face options. They look weird to me. But I like the animals. I guess the whale is like, *Here's a cute thing to make you smile.* That's all. *I'm thinking of you and want to brighten up your day,* or whatever. Isn't that obvious?"

"No one uses the whale, Mom. No one knows what you mean when you send it."

"Well, it doesn't matter," said Rebecca. "It's still adorable. I'll see you in six and a half hours. 'Kay? I gotta finish packing. Hug hug."

"Whale."

"What? Oh yes. Whale to you too."

Adelaide spent the rest of the day dozing with her wrist elevated. Texting Stacey with her left hand.

She dreaded seeing Toby, whom she hadn't seen since his relapse, but she found that she did want to see her mother. There was something about being hurt that made her long for Rebecca's comforting frizzy hair and wool smell, annoying as she was so much of the time.

At four o'clock, the two of them arrived, frazzled and tired, having hit terrible traffic. "I'm making brownies," said Rebecca, who was wearing a hat of fuzzy red yarn despite the heat. She'd lugged a grocery bag from the car. "I couldn't think of anything I could do that would actually be of any use. But I know Adelaide is a sucker for brownies, so we stopped and bought ingredients."

"You could have texted me. I would have bought them," said Levi.

"I was driving," she said. "I didn't even think of it." She shoved her bag of groceries into his arms and then leaned against him for a moment.

Then she grabbed Adelaide and squeezed her in an enormous

mommy hug. "I hate that freaking dog," she said. "I can't stand it that this happened to you."

"She's a good dog," said Adelaide. "I'm not mad at her."

The boy, Jack, had stayed with Adelaide until Levi pulled up in his car. She had felt incredibly grateful for his shirtless rescue. She had described it to Stacey in precise, objectifying detail.

But she hadn't forgotten that he'd taken the time to clip B-Cake to her leash. Or probably had. And with the pain she was in, and her anxiety about seeing Toby again, Jack hadn't actually been the center of Adelaide's thoughts.

Toby was climbing out of the car, looking heavier and taller than last time she'd seen him. The wispy mustache was gone. He hugged her.

"Hi."

"Hi."

"Poop weiner thunder-butt," he said, looking at her bandage. "That dog really nommed you."

She nodded.

He hugged her again. She patted him gently with her good hand, not really hugging back.

"I'm so sorry, Adelaide," he said. "I'm so, so sorry. I have been just the worst version of myself. I hope we can start over."

"I don't know," she whispered, pulling back. Their parents had gone into the house.

"I get it," he said. "But I'm doing all my programs and I just wonder, could we hang out this weekend? I was thinking about it on the drive up. Could we, I don't know, walk around the campus? Or go see a movie? Something without Mom and Dad?"

Adelaide didn't want to. "I don't have a lot of energy right now," she told him. "I lost blood and I'm on antibiotics and all that."

"Just play Unstable Unicorns, even. I packed the cards. Just for twenty minutes, maybe?"

She didn't think her brother should ask *anything* of her. Not even twenty minutes of her time. "Maybe," she told him. "I'll see how I feel."

"Just one game. Or a walk," Toby said. "Then if you don't want to stay in touch with me after that, we can go back to just seeing each other at holidays, being at arm's length or whatever. As long as it takes."

"Toby."

"I get it. You have a very good right to be mad at me."

"I'm not mad at all."

"You *are* mad, Adelaide."

"I'm not," she told him. "You have a disease. There's an epidemic. You have susceptible brain chemistry."

"I think you're mad."

"Don't tell me how I feel!" she shouted. "I'm not mad! I forgive you!"

"Okay, but you don't ever talk to me," he said. "You don't talk to me, but you text these shallow little nothing texts, and we used to—I don't know. You used to be my sister, Adelaide."

"What the hell do you want?" she said, the force of her voice surprising her. "I reached out to you, over and over. After you went to the hospital. I did. I sent you

letters and pictures and

you never wrote back. I

234

tried to talk to you. I

gave you my cacti and

all those damn Lego dioramas, and you

didn't even

seem to

notice. I gave you

my bedroom. I don't have anywhere to sleep at home

anymore, and I

saved your

damn life,

and all you did in response to any of it was turn

cold and

say nothing and

think about yourself. And then you relapsed, which

ripped us all apart, Toby.

I don't think you can have any idea how it

ripped me apart. I didn't want to tell anyone. I only told my

roommate. Not because I was

ashamed. I wasn't

ashamed. But because I was so

desperate, so

overwhelmingly worried and

ruined over it, and so

angry that it was impossible to let it out in any way

whatsoever, because it felt like if I let it out I might literally

trash a classroom or

hurt someone or

set something on fire, so I just

shut my mouth, and now

you're complaining about my freaking texts being shallow? Can you even hear yourself?"

She stopped to take a breath. Her wrist hurt, her heart hurt, and her brother was standing there in front of her, taking her rage.

"I know I got to have you as a sister because up to a point, I was a decent brother," Toby said after a minute. "And you could love me when I was like that. It wasn't fair that I turned into an effing werewolf."

Adelaide smiled. In spite of herself.

"It's almost impossible to love a werewolf," Toby went on. "I hate that I am one, I really do hate it with all my guts, but I have to just live with it, you know? I have to live with knowing I am capable of all that badness, and just figure out how not to do it again, and it would be so much easier— No, I don't want to say that. It's not your job to keep me sober. I just mean, it would be— I would be so much happier— No, it's not your job to make me happy, either. I just. I want to be your brother again. Adelaide, you are the only person I really like spending time with who knows all the terrible stuff about me there is to know. With everyone else I have to hide it or explain myself. Confess. Then put them at ease. Which is almost impossible. And—I just want you to try hanging out with me on this trip. For a short time. If that's okay. Please. Would you?"

Adelaide looked at Toby. He was crying. He did it like he used to do it when he was small, contorting his mouth and not covering his face, snorting the snot back up his nose. It was disgusting and Adelaide loved it about him.

"Okay," she said. "I can do that."

"Really?"

"Yeah. I'll play a freaking card game with you, you little dweeb."

"Okay. Okay, good."

Toby wiped his face. He got his bag from the backseat. He and Adelaide went inside and helped Rebecca make brownies.

Then they all watched a cooking show.

Rebecca knitted. Toby put his feet on the coffee table. When the show was over, Levi and Toby went out to pick up Chinese food. Adelaide and her mother walked the dogs.

The four of them ate noodles and chicken with garlic sauce, sitting outside on the porch and watching the sun set over the Alabaster campus.

Toby and Adelaide played Unstable Unicorns.

Mikey Double L texted late that night.

Hi. Thinking about you.

Adelaide thought awhile before answering. She had hidden her pain from Mikey Double L from day one of their relationship, and still he had sensed it and pulled away from it.

She might as well lay the truth out for him. There was nothing to lose.

Recovering from a pit-bull
mauling. Hospital. Whole bit.

And my ex-junkie brother is
here. First time I have seen
him since his relapse. Intense
day.

Sorry I never told you about
Toby. But it has been a thing.
All year.

. . .

. . .

Whoa. That's good he is
recovering, though.

Are you okay?

I'm okay.

I love him and I'm furious and
I don't trust him.

But I can tell he loves me.

So, y'know. We are figuring it
out.

What happened with the pit
bull?

. . .

. . .

Adelaide started to compose the story.

But then, she didn't want to tell Mikey about meeting Jack.

So she rewrote the story, leaving Jack out of it.

And then she realized: *I don't have to tell this story to Mikey, at all. He is not my Mikey Double L anymore.*

I don't owe him an explanation. For anything.

So she didn't write an answer.

She turned her phone off and went to sleep.

26

THE PHILOSOPHICAL PARTY, REVISITED

"This is my lover's house," said Kaspian-Lee as the philosophers milled around the kitchen, pouring themselves wine and saying words like *hermeneutical, etiology,* and *supervenience.* "I am entitled to go into the freezer. I'm not being rude." She took out some ice and dragged Adelaide to the cheese plate, where she made rude remarks about the partygoers and pushed Adelaide to try the Morbier.

Then she turned abruptly to a tall, heavy young man, only about seventeen, wearing a blue button-down with the sleeves rolled up. He had curling dark hair, dramatic eyebrows, huge brown eyes, tan skin, and dimpled cheeks. His nose was prominent and had a bump in it. "Will you play?" Kaspian-Lee asked him. There was lipstick on the rim of her plastic cup.

The young man shrugged. "If you want."

"I do want," she said. "Adelaide, this is Oscar. He's here to play the piano."

"Hi, Adelaide."

"Hi, Oscar."

"What happened to your wrist?" he asked.

"An argument with a pit bull."

"Really?"

"Really."

"I like pit bulls," he said. "Can I still like pit bulls?"

"Yeah," she said. "It was only a misunderstanding."

Oscar headed toward the piano but got waylaid by a short, sweaty philosopher who asked whether he thought hell existed. Adelaide stole the Brie and scuttled off with it to a corner by the bookshelf.

She was

conscious

of herself in the room, as if

she were looking down on the party from above.

She was

conscious

of her short dress and

of her youth, which felt like it oozed out of her pores.

She watched Oscar. He held his hands behind his back as he spoke, leaning down to hear the short philosopher. When he extricated himself, he still didn't play the piano right away. Instead, he ate some grapes and came over to where Adelaide was standing.

"Is that the Brie you're holding?" he asked.

"Yes." Adelaide felt her face heat up.

"You took the entire official Martin Schlegel Brie?"

"Yes."

"God, that is so brave."

"Do you want some?"

"I do."

"Here."

"Do I just— Oh, ah, oh. Yeah. That is a serious cheese."

"Don't eat it all," said Adelaide.

"I wouldn't dream of it.

"This is a strange party," Oscar said, leaning against the bookshelf and looking out. "I don't think I've been to a party full of academics before."

"Me neither."

"Why did you come?"

"This college student I met by the vending machines invited me. Perla. Why did *you* come?"

"Kaspian-Lee is friends with my mother. She heard me at a concert last year and asked if I'd come play piano. She's paying me."

"Are all adult parties like this?" Adelaide asked. "Are we doomed to a life of terrible parties when we grow up?"

"Possibly. But I think we will throw better parties."

"Let's pretend we're on safari. Imagine we're looking at the philosophers through binoculars and they're not philosophers, they're meerkats."

Oscar held his hands up to his eyes like binoculars.

"No!" Adelaide grabbed his fingers. "You can't let them see your binoculars. Philosophers frighten easily."

They leaned against the kitchen counter and looked. There were philosophers in the kitchen, and beyond that, in the dining room and living room. Some were in the hallway, waiting for the bathroom.

"Look," said Oscar. "They cross their legs when they're nervous."

"They look each other in the eye a lot. It's probably a dominance behavior."

"Yes, yes. That one just cowed the other one, do you see them on the couch? He made her look away."

"Uh-huh."

"Look how they chew their food. It's so cute."

"I wish I could have one for a pet."

"You'd have to get two. They get lonely if they're solo."

"I do this all the time," she told him.

"Pretend you're on safari?"

"In line at the coffee shop or in a boring class. In the supermarket I pretend I'm observing animals in the wild and that I'm lucky to get to look at them. Like it's a once-in-a-lifetime experience."

"I like that, Adelaide," he said.

Kaspian-Lee appeared next to them. "Now is a good time," she said authoritatively.

Oscar took a suit jacket off the piano bench and put it on, despite the heat. He sat down and began to play.

Adelaide had never thought about the piano in her life. She had never listened to classical music. But he rained on the keys with an enormous concentration.

The music was turbulent. It made her feel as if the sky were about to break open, and as if

Mikey not loving her and

Toby being an addict

were being pushed through the music

into the sky, and as if somehow Oscar

knew how she felt,

knew the storm that was in her.

The philosophers gathered round, their conversation hushed.

B-Cake flopped on the rug with her belly up.

Oscar, this magical Oscar, made music. The whole room listened. He seemed like he couldn't see anything but the piano. Once the piece began, his hands led the way.

The song ended.

Someone said it was a sonata. Adelaide felt dizzy.

She went to Oscar's side. "Would you want to take a walk with me?" she said. "I'm not consenting to anything."

"I'd love to," said Oscar. "I'm not consenting to anything either."

27

A ROGUE GAME
OF CARDS

"What's the best party you ever went to?" asked Oscar as they walked. "Since that was obviously the worst."

Adelaide thought. "A party on a roof in Boston. Someone was projecting movies onto the wall of the building opposite, and there were paper lanterns strung across. I met a boy and I felt magical and, I don't know, sophisticated. What about you?"

"A party at music camp," he said, "last summer when I was a counselor in training. We took beer out into this field in the back of camp. Someone drove a pickup truck out there and left it running with the doors open so we had music. Everybody danced in the field in the dark. We knew we'd get in huge trouble if we got caught, because of the alcohol, but we blasted the music anyway."

"You went to music summer camp?"

"Seven years."

"How come you're not there now?"

"Junior counselor only pays a hundred dollars a week. I wanted to make more money. I have a job at Uncle Benny's Fine Sandwiches. Hey, are you any good at cards?"

"I'm amazing."

"Are you really?"

"I've played a lot. My little brother used to be a huge gamer. We'd bring a deck of cards with us to restaurants."

"Then come on."

They were in town now, and Oscar veered into a juice bar Adelaide had never gone into before. Its lights were on and there was a woman behind the counter, but there wasn't a lot of juicing going on at ten p.m. Oscar waved to the woman and pushed through a door at the back.

They walked into a coffee shop, dark and lined with old couches. It smelled of espresso and dust. There was a small counter, and a menu that featured homemade marshmallows and eighteen kinds of tea.

"Let me buy you a marshmallow," said Oscar.

"If I can buy you a tea."

"It's a deal."

They found a pair of low armchairs with a glass coffee table between them and surveyed a shelf of worn board games.

"Let's just play cards," said Adelaide. "That's what we planned on."

They sat opposite one another and played Crazy Eights.

Oscar kept claiming he knew rules that didn't exist. "I'm setting down my eight," he said, "but then I'm invoking the revoking clause, so I take it up again, and then, fish, fish, turkey, striped turkey, and there—I only have one card left, and it's my eight, so I'm going to win."

"You are not going to win."

"I am. I have an eight left and I can definitely play an eight, so I'm going to win."

"I'm invoking British Policeman."

"What does that mean?"

"Come on. You don't know the British Policeman rule?" Adelaide put down the king of diamonds. "I play the British Policeman, and you have to take up all the cards you played on the last play." Oscar took them up and she put down a two. "Now this is Cutlery Ping Ping, which means because it's a two, you have to draw two additional cards from the pile."

"Nope! 'Cause I'm playing Flippity Flop, then Freudian Bitch."

"Then I'll do Citibike. And Double Citibike."

"Anglerfish. Dog. Fight! Fight!"

"Disco Is Dead."

"Snake in the Grass."

"Four snakes. It's a Swamp."

"Malibu Dancer."

"No, no. You have to draw," she said. "You can't play Malibu Dancer after a Swamp."

Oscar stood up and came over to her armchair then. He squashed himself in next to her. "I have to kiss you now," he said. "If that's okay. Because nobody has ever taught me British Policeman before. I'm going to be such a better Crazy Eights player after this."

"Okay," she said.

And they kissed right there in the café, and Oscar's lips were soft and questioning and he one hundred percent knew what he was doing.

28

A MINIATURIST

And in this universe, Adelaide Buchwald fell slowly and gently in love with Oscar Moretti. She loved him far from perfectly. There isn't a perfect way to love anyway. But she did not hide the misery in the center of her chest, and she did not fixate on what they meant to one another. Oscar made it easy. He wasn't trying to be anything he wasn't, like an ideal boyfriend; and he wasn't trying to escape anything, like grief.

She told him about Toby. She told him about her academic probation. She let him see her ugly beige bra and it was all fine.

She began to build her design for *Fool for Love*, a solid gold motel room with a giant bed on the wall and skeletons entwined in the dirt underneath.

She texted her brother. Since his visit, something had cleared between them.

Every day, Adelaide walked the dogs. Even Rabbit, who wore her muzzle.

She had her dog bites disinfected.

One night, someone stole her bike from in front of the Factory. Jack,

the boy she'd met that one time in the dog run,

the boy from the rooftop party back in Boston,

the boy who'd punched Rabbit in the face and stanched her wounds by going shirtless,

drove by and picked her up in his car.

He was still beautiful to the point that he made her dizzy, but Adelaide didn't kiss him.

She just looked at him a lot, thanked him for the ride, and got out of the car.

He wasn't that interesting to talk to anyway.

Oscar was waiting for her on the steps of her dad's house. He came upstairs and stayed until two in the morning. They held each other and loved each other in the dark, and then they turned on the lights and watched a movie together, eating sandy shortbread cookies straight out of the box.

Adelaide worked on the model some more.

She texted her brother some more too.

She hung out with Terrance and Oscar some days, and when Stacey came to visit, the four of them went swimming at Dodson's Hole, then stayed up late playing pinball at Luigi's. One night she brought Oscar to the film series the philosophers had organized. Terrance agreed to come too. They brought bags of Doritos and sodas from the vending machines. Adelaide and Oscar held hands. Walking out of the auditorium, they ran into

Perla and her friend Yael. They all sat around on the edge of the entryway fountain, talking about Catherine Deneuve and Roman Polanski, sharing the giant bag of peanut M&M's Perla had brought to the movie.

Adelaide met Oscar's parents, who ran an antiques store together. They had her over for a dinner of cold pasta and two weird salads. Oscar's room was chaotic. He did his own laundry and draped his clothes into piles when they were clean. There were piles of towels and bed linens too, many of them sitting on his bed. His curtains flapped in the breeze. Some nights, when his parents were out, Oscar made Adelaide bowls of pasta with red sauce and shook hot pepper flakes onto it. They ate on the couch, watching videos.

One day, Oscar came to Kaspian-Lee's classroom. He looked at the model Adelaide was working on. "It's so meticulous," he said, quite serious.

"Is that a good thing?"

"Yes."

"I've been obsessed."

"I'm awestruck. It's so strange and beautiful. And you're a miniaturist."

Then he kissed her, and it was like he was kissing her brain.

She kissed his brain back. The next day she made him a Lego diorama with a piano in it. The person playing the piano was Lego Batman.

Oscar worked at the sandwich shop most days. He didn't want Adelaide to come by and talk to him while he worked. He said it was embarrassing and distracting when he was trying to do a good job.

She said that was insulting.

He said, "Please, just let me concentrate at work."

He said, "It's my thing. I don't come to the classroom and watch you build your model."

He said, "No, it's not that I care more about sandwiches than you, it's that I'm concentrating. I'm taking orders. I can't do that and have a conversation, or *host your afternoon* so that you're not bored. If we don't have customers, I'm supposed to be cleaning the counters."

He said, "It's not girlfriend time in the sandwich shop!"

Adelaide said, "I'd be *happy* if you came to the classroom. But you don't *want* to come."

She said, "You could come on your days off, do stuff on your laptop or whatever."

She said, "Am I your girlfriend?"

He said, "I'm all in, I am, but I don't think you should come to my job, that's all. Let's have some boundaries, for god's sake."

He said, "Yes, you're my girlfriend. You absolutely are. But no Uncle Benny's. Please."

They had quite an argument.

Oscar showed up at Kaspian-Lee's classroom the next day, on his break from the sandwich shop. He had run over and he was breathing hard. In his hands he had a Lego kit called Heartlake City Pet Center. It had tiny Lego dogs and included a vet clinic and a grooming parlor. He gave it to Adelaide and then ran back to work.

Adelaide wanted Oscar not because he had suffered and not because he was beautiful. Although she did find him beautiful.

And she didn't want him because he fit an idea in her head that was labeled *boyfriend*. In many ways, he didn't fit.

She saw him clearly, with no distortion.

She wanted him, also, because he loved something else so much: his music.

Some evenings, Oscar holed up playing piano in a soundproof room in his family's basement. Adelaide thought about him those nights, teetering on something like obsession, thinking about his hands on the piano, the way he gave the instrument his complete attention.

29

YOU COULD LET THAT
IMAGINARY VERSION GO

Many weeks into the summer, Adelaide finished the model and showed it to Kaspian-Lee.

"When you tell me how hard you worked, you miss the point," said the teacher. "The work you put in is irrelevant. The result is what matters."

"I think the work people put in *is* relevant," Adelaide said, putting a protective hand on her model. "The process of making something changes a person."

"It is not an A-grade design," said the teacher. "It's self-indulgent."

"Ms. Kaspian-Lee?"

"Yes."

"We could talk about
why it's gold, and
why the bed is where it is, and
why the dirt is out the window.

No matter how much you hate it, you could take the time to *see* it, instead of complaining that

my design doesn't measure up to the

imaginary A-grade design that's in your mind.

You could let that

imaginary version

go and

see what's in front of you."

Kaspian-Lee sighed. "Your glue is very neat and everything is to scale and level."

"Thank you."

They were silent for a moment.

"Perhaps," said Kaspian-Lee finally. "Perhaps I have neglected to tell you that I think there's something unique about your vision for this play. I have given this assignment for four years in a row. Your gold motel room with its desperately sad, unusable throne of a bed, it's not a workable set. It doesn't serve Shephard's text. But it is *something*. In fact, it made me both feel and think. Are you taking sculpture senior year?"

"I haven't registered yet."

"Take sculpture. The instructor is good. And then take my puppet-building course."

Adelaide nodded.

"I apologize," said Kaspian-Lee. "I have been dealing with an extreme situation in my personal life. Shall we call it a B-plus, with points off for self-indulgence and failure to serve the play? I'll submit your grade to the office."

+ + +

Adelaide took the model home. She lit it carefully. She took photographs of it.

Her phone pinged.

There was a text from Mikey Double L. It was a picture.

They were dressed for the spring formal.

Another picture, a selfie of the two of them kissing.

And then a third text:

Us.

The phone rang.

"I miss you," Mikey said when she answered.

"Hi, Mikey."

"I owe you seventeen apologies. I wish I could see you right now and say everything that needs saying in person. It's so awkward on the phone."

"I was on academic probation last term," Adelaide said.

"You were?"

"I never wanted to tell you. And I didn't do my work. I had to get an extension in Set Design. I just finished my project defense with Kaspian-Lee."

"How did it go?"

"I'm proud of it, actually."

"I love you," said Mikey.

"What?"

"I made a terrible mistake, breaking up with you."

Adelaide didn't say anything. She kind of wanted to talk about her model some more.

"I'm such an idiot," Mikey said. "It was just stupid. I got scared of being together all summer. Without our friends. It seemed too intense."

"That's nice of you to say, Mikey."

"It's the truth. I was scared of being connected, I think. Of love."

Adelaide sat down on the floor. She noticed her arms had light sprinkles of gold from carrying the model. She and Mikey were silent on the phone.

"I don't think it *was* a mistake to break up," she said finally. "I wasn't happy."

"You weren't? You seemed happy."

"I thought I was happy."

"Isn't that the same thing? I'm sorry, Adelaide. Please tell me I haven't ruined everything between us forever."

"You can think you're happy and not be happy."

"Could I come see you this weekend? Could we talk about it? I miss you so much."

"I don't think so."

"Just to talk."

"No."

Mikey paused. "Is there another guy?"

"Yeah," she said. "There is."

"And this other guy, he makes you happy?"

"It's not his job to make me happy," she told him.

Adelaide didn't often think of Mikey after that.
    She texted her brother more and more, and
    as the summer went on, she began to trust that the
    Toby she knew now was Toby.

256

That he could stay sober.

That he genuinely wanted to, and had the tools.

That they could be

brother and

sister in

something of the way they once had been.

Or in some other way, some way they hadn't invented yet.

The last two weeks of the summer, Oscar's parents were taking him on vacation. They weren't going far; it was about three hours to Maine, where relatives had a house. It was okay. Adelaide knew he'd be back at the start of the school year.

She wouldn't be returning to Baltimore until Thanksgiving break. Some of the dogs needed her until move-in day on campus.

She said goodbye to Oscar the night before he left. They stood on her porch and he hugged her long and tight.

"It's not goodbye," Adelaide said.

"It's not."

"Hello."

"Hello."

Then they made out like the lucky young people they were, until Oscar's curfew.

30

A BATTLE OF
SURPASSING
RIDICULOUSNESS

Toby came to visit. The plan was that he'd stay with Adelaide
and Levi for a week, and at the end of that, Rebecca would come
for a short time, then drive Toby home to Baltimore. In the
meantime, she would visit a friend in Boston.

When Adelaide picked up Toby at the bus stop, he had only
a backpack with him, no suitcase. She offered to take the pack,
but he said it was fine. It wasn't heavy.

She didn't know what to talk about in person. In a rush, her
fear for Toby came back, that he would

hurt himself again, that he would

not be

okay,

that the disease would

take him over when he came off the bus.

He seemed so young. She could see the

little boy he used to be, in his face. She thought,

We shouldn't be allowed to have him here.

He's away from his sponsor and his appointments.

Mom shouldn't have let him come.

What if he gets into trouble on my watch? What if he relapses and it's my fault?

He held up a bag from a doughnut shop. It was squashed. "There were doughnuts at the bus station layover," he said. "I got you Boston cream." He opened the bag and peeked in side. "The cream has blooped out, though."

Adelaide took the bag and looked inside. "It's the worse for wear," she said. "But I could eat it."

"It's a couple hours old," said Toby. "I've been on the bus for a while."

She tore off a hunk of doughnut and tasted it. "I'm super into it," she told him. "Thank you."

She walked him down to the lake. Toby took off his shoes and waded in. Adelaide did too, though no one ever swam in the lake. It wasn't allowed.

"Can we have a zucchini battle?" asked Toby. "While I'm here."

"For real?"

"Yeah. I feel like it might be nice to just solidly whack each other with vegetables. For old times' sake."

"I guess we can."

"Maybe carrots, instead of zucchini," he said. "I feel like a carrot battle might work even better."

"You're on."

The next day, Toby and Adelaide finished painting Levi's

bathroom and the hall. Toby was a sloppy painter, though. Adelaide didn't let him do the trim. He did cleanup and made sandwich runs.

The day it was complete, they walked to the supermarket while Levi was at work. They planned to take a cab back. It was icy inside the store. There was a buzz from the white lights. The broccoli there was sad and yellow at the tips. Levi had given them money, and Toby chose all kinds of food Adelaide would never have thought about: granola with dried blueberries, multiple mangoes, cake mix and a tub of fake-vanilla frosting, pasta sauce with spicy peppers.

They got four extra-long carrots for a battle (two weapons and two backups). Then they got inspired and added two eggplants, two seedless cucumbers, and two heads of tragic broccoli.

Adelaide texted Oscar, who was in Maine.

> My brother and I are staging a
> vegetable battle.

Nice.

> We can't decide on a
> soundtrack.

Are you thinking classical
or pop?

Well, it's a comedy.

It would be funny with
serious music.

Are you filming it?

. . .

Yes, filming. We just decided,
but yes.

Maybe some of it in slow
motion, Toby says.

Then you'll edit the score in
later.

The question for now is,
what is the set design?

Toby says a location shoot in
Dad's backyard.

Oh! Wait!

The vegetable battle will be
staged in my solid gold set
model for Fool for Love.

Perfection.

Re: score. I think Chariots
of Fire.

        It's so hot when you say score
        instead of music.

Ha.

        What is Chariots of Fire?

Good music for a vegetable
battle. Classical-ISH.
But not.

        (Opening app. Listening)

        I just played Toby the Chariots
        of Fire soundtrack and he is
        laughing so hard he knocked
        over several oranges. They
        went rolling through the
        produce department.

        Now he is in danger of
        knocking over a watermelon.

        Oh damn. The watermelon is
        down. Rolling!

The manager just came over and said that we should not pollute the airspace of the Stop & Shop with our music and that is just basic manners.

And I was like, but it's Chariots of Fire!

And he was like, watermelons and oranges are not toys. They are fruits, and there is a price on them, and this is a place for serious shopping behavior.

Did he really say "behavior"?

No.

I can help w/film if you want.

We have to do it before Toby leaves.

I could come tomorrow.

From Maine? Would you seriously?

I would.

I would come to see you,
Adelaide.

I want to see you.

They were unloading the groceries at the house by the time
Adelaide got to Oscar's "I would."

She did want him to come help them make a movie.

She wanted him to take her,

just her,

down to the lake at the edge of the campus, underneath the
big old oak tree, and

press her up against the rough bark.

She wanted him to push against her as the temperature
dropped and the moon went up into the sky.

She wanted to take his shirt off in the cold night air and have
him stand there shivering before her, to let her touch him with
her warm hands, her nails painted blue, their breaths loud.

She wanted Oscar to play the *Chariots of Fire* song for her on
the piano, and to help her move her things out of storage and
into her new dorm room, the single she'd have for senior year,
hanging fairy lights around her window.

She wanted him to adore Toby, and she wanted Toby to adore
him, and for Oscar and her to start the school year together,
finding one another Friday nights as soon as classes were
done, playing ridiculous invented card games in the secret café
behind the juice bar. She wanted to lie on the floor in his living

room, listening to him play piano and doing her homework. To eat weird salads with his parents and to talk late into the night and—

Adelaide wanted Oscar to come down from Maine so that she could believe, as she had believed with Mikey, that this thing between them was permanent.

He'd surpass Mikey Double L, become more legitimate than Mikey had ever been, because he, Oscar, had made the gesture to come back for her, the gesture Mikey never would have made.

That wasn't a good reason for Oscar to come.

Toby and Adelaide put away the food. They stored the vegetables for their film in gallon-size Ziploc bags.

Then they ate potato chips and watched old *Saturday Night Live* episodes until six.

They walked Lord Voldemort and the Great God Pan. All the other dogs had been reclaimed by their owners, who were back from summer vacation.

As they walked past EllaBella's house, the dog looked at Adelaide from her spot at the window. Just her soft black head peeked over the ledge.

"That's EllaBella," Adelaide told Toby. "She was with me all summer."

"She has a good face," said Toby. "I remember her photo. Can we take her out?"

Voldemort and GG Pan turned instinctively toward Ella-Bella's door.

Adelaide rang the bell.

Mr. Byrd answered barefoot. He wore jeans and black-rimmed glasses. She could see his suitcases were still in the hall, even though he'd been home for three days. EllaBella wagged.

"Adelaide. Hi. EllaBella's glad to see you."

"This is my brother, Toby."

"Hello, Toby." The teacher reached out and shook hands. "And who are these guys?"

He knelt, and GG Pan snarfled his face while Lord Voldemort hid shyly behind Adelaide's legs.

It seemed so strange that Derrick Byrd had never even seen these dogs. They were EllaBella's friends.

"Could we take EllaBella to the dog run?" she asked.

"You want to? I just walked her."

"I miss her," Adelaide said. "And Toby wants to meet her."

Toby nodded.

"Come in for a second while I find her leash."

They followed him into his house, which Adelaide had been in so many times without him. Pieces of it seemed out of place. Books had migrated across countertops and into smaller piles. There was a half-eaten plate of Nutella on toast next to a laptop. Byrd was—Adelaide glanced at his work—prepping a course on precolonial African history.

He bent down to attach the leash to EllaBella's collar. "Let me get your key for you again," he said. "I'm going out at seven."

He tried pay her for the walk, but Adelaide told him this one was on the house.

At the dog run, Adelaide and Toby ate cough drops she had in her backpack, even though they didn't have sore throats.

Toby threw a stick for Voldemort and GG Pan while EllaBella trotted around with her nose to the ground, wagging her tail faintly.

Texts.

> Oscar. I'm sorry, but please
>
> wait
>
> and come back from Maine on Sunday.
>
> Not tomorrow.

...

...

> Hey. Did you get my earlier text?
>
> I don't know if you bought a bus ticket already or anything.

I didn't buy a bus ticket.

Yet.

Did you change your mind
about making the movie?

No.

. . .

. . .

I want to make the movie.

I love that you offered your
help.

But

I need to just hang out with my
brother.

It's like, we forgot we knew
each other, forgot we were
ever siblings, and we have
only now recognized each
other again.

It feels important.

Family time. I get it.

My parents weren't happy
about me going anyway.

                    I want to see you. I wish you
                    were here.

?

You just told me not to
come, Adelaide.

                    Sorry. I know.

                    . . .

                    . . .

                    Please don't come. I need the
                    time with Toby. XOXO

Okay.

31

THE WAVE OF LOVE

Toby and Adelaide went swimming in the pool and hit each other with brightly colored foam noodles. They got take-out Chinese food and walked around campus eating lo mein out of cardboard containers.

They shot the vegetable battle on Adelaide's phone.

The battle was vigorous and bloody.

The golden *Fool for Love* set model did not survive the process. Bits of broccoli got all over it. And carrot grime. And the ketchup they used for blood. One wall fell down.

It was okay. It was an impermanent object. The summer was over, and it was time for the model to die. They filmed the wreckage as well.

The next day, they argued about how to edit the film. How to score it. Whether there should be subtitles.

They didn't finish it that day, or the day after.

They got distracted. The new ninth graders showed up for three days' orientation, and could be seen walking around wearing Alabaster T-shirts and lanyards on their necks, clustering together, holding maps. Rebecca drove up and Levi's summer position in Admissions ended and he got a couple of days off to spend time with the family.

Rebecca was laid up with sciatica after the drive, but she emerged from the bedroom for dinner and kept hugging Adelaide sideways the way parents do when they want to be all nurturing but not intrusive. The next day, everyone helped Adelaide move her stuff into the new dorm room.

They hung fairy lights around her window. Rebecca gave Adelaide a new set of sheets wrapped in gift paper. And she opened the trunk of the car to reveal eight Lego dioramas, carefully packed in Bubble Wrap for the trip. They set them up on Adelaide's bookshelf after photographing them in some decent light. "Just in case you want them for your college-application portfolio," Levi said.

The four of them went for pizza on Toby and Rebecca's last night.

"If she keeps touching my face I might vomit," Adelaide whispered to Toby between bites. "It's super oppressive."

"She's always trying to touch my face too," he whispered back. "She does it when she's feeling the wave of love."

"I really want her to stop."

"Just let her do it," Toby said. "Just breathe until it's over. She's the mom. You were gone all year. It makes her happy."

"Look at them, whispering on their side of the table, just like when they were kids," said Rebecca.

"Some things never change," said Levi.

But they had changed.

Adelaide would

never be the same. Toby would

never be the same either.

They could not go back to what they once had been.

They could only go forward.

Rebecca insisted on going to the drugstore after dinner. While Adelaide and Toby looked at enormous Toblerones and various types of Goldfish crackers, their mother filled two shopping baskets with what looked like a year's supply of apricot body lotion, razors, Advil, shampoo, conditioner, toothpaste, ChapStick, tampons, panty liners, and condoms.

"I'm glad you have my lady parts taken care of so thoroughly," said Adelaide, looking in the basket.

"I'm not asking your business, but I want you to have them," said Rebecca, about the condoms. "Safety is very important."

"People are going to think I'm a hoarder."

"We'll get a bin for under your bed," said Rebecca. "I'm a thorough shopper. You like that about me."

"Yeah, I do, I guess," said Adelaide.

32

SOMEDAY, OR IN ANOTHER UNIVERSE

Adelaide was in her dorm room when Oscar called.

Oscar said he didn't know how to tell her this.

Oscar said he was sorry.

Oscar said he wasn't coming back.

Not ever.

"I need you to explain this to me," she said. The room swirled around her. She lay down.

And Oscar explained.

It was music. His name had been pulled off the wait list at one of the music conservatories he'd applied to. It was in Michigan. There was financial aid.

So Oscar was going. It was his senior year. It would make a huge difference for him, applying to college. And he wanted to be there. To live in a world of music, to breathe it, to have his mind expanded, to think differently, to play differently.

"When did you find out?" Adelaide asked him.

"A week ago," he said. "I found out a week ago."

"Before you offered to come see me?"

"Yeah. That was why I wanted to come so badly."

"Why didn't you tell me right then?"

"I wanted to. I wrote ten different texts telling you, but they were all horrible. And I called, but when you picked up you were watching that movie with Toby. Remember? Then I got scared."

"Scared of what?"

"Losing you. I wanted to put it off," said Oscar. "Because it's awful."

"Yeah," she told him. "It is awful."

"I have to go," he said. "I want to go."

And of course,

of course,

he did have to go. He should want to go.

"When I told you not to come, I thought we had a whole year in front of us," Adelaide told Oscar. "I needed to be with my brother."

"You did."

"I thought you'd be back."

"I have to go straight from Maine so I can be there on time. Tomorrow, actually. My mom will send the rest of my stuff."

"Tomorrow is very soon."

"I'll be back at winter break."

"But I'll be in Baltimore."

"I know. I thought of that."

"It's more than a thousand miles away. I might not ever see you again."

"I might not ever see you either," Oscar said.

She loved him. She wanted everything for him, everything that he hoped for. "Twenty years from now, you'll see me," she told him.

"I will?"

"I'll run into you in New York City, by chance, you know? In a movie theater. I'll be there with my kids,

and my husband, and

we'll be taking the children to see a serious philosophy film, or else a film about Lego people having adventures.

I'll have a wedge of Brie in my bag. Wrapped in plastic so it doesn't smell up my purse. You'll be standing in the lobby with your gorgeous spouse, talking to this eager old guy who's a music fan. He stopped you in the lobby because he saw you

play the piano

at

Carnegie Hall

and it changed his life.

He can't believe he's seeing you in the cinema, holding a handful of buttery popcorn.

You'll catch my eye."

"My wife will be jealous."

"Maybe she will. And you'll wonder

if it's me or

if it's someone who reminds you of

me,

and I'll wonder

if it's you or

if it's someone who reminds me of

you,

and you'll say, *Excuse me, I can't talk to you about Beethoven any longer, good sir, because Adelaide Buchwald is here and she's old but still super attractive.*"

"I don't want us to have spouses," said Oscar. "Can we be single?"

"Okay."

"Single but not like, lonely and sad about it."

"All right. We're single. And

at first I objectify the hell out of you, because I'm just thinking, *Oh, look at that*

fine hunk of a man with the masterful hands and

the amazing profile, but then I realize it's

you,

the Oscar of my youth."

"Do I have all my hair?" asked Oscar. "My dad is bald, and I'd like to have all my hair in this story."

"You're only thirty-seven. You have all your hair. And I have adorable children with me, but I'm divorced, so don't worry about that. My kids are old enough to go sit in the movie theater alone. I'm wearing fantastic clothes and I'm in New York for an

exhibition of my miniaturist dollhouses

filled with dramatizations of famous murders, or possibly for

a film festival that's showing my

stop-motion animation masterpiece."

"That sounds like art you would make," said Oscar.

"I know it does," said Adelaide. "I think I'd make an awesome series of dollhouse murder sites."

"What's your stop-motion masterpiece?"

She considered. "It's about dogs who have inner lives, like people, but they're also kind of dogs. You know? They talk a lot about shoe leather and urination."

"I don't think I'll wonder if it's you," said Oscar. "I'll know it's you. I'll always know it's you, even if you're old."

"You know it's me," said Adelaide. "And I know it's you.

We sit on a red leather bench in the lobby while my children watch the movie.

We're adults, and we have lived a lot of the things there are to live."

"I'm very glad to see you," said Oscar softly.

"I'm very glad to see you too. It seems like old times."

"It seems like old times."

He was crying on the phone.

"You're going to go make beautiful art and have a huge adventure, Oscar," Adelaide told him. "I want you to do it. You deserve to do it. But also, I wish you'd stay."

"I wish I'd stay, too," said Oscar. "I can't imagine a time when I won't love you and want you."

Goodbye.

33

THINGS SHE COULD NOT
EXPRESS WITH WORDS

Adelaide lay awake for a bit after she hung up. She was filled with love and sadness, and the two emotions swirled around each other. She felt like her chest had more room in it than it used to. Then she fell asleep and it was morning.

She took a shower and cried under the water.

She cried for the loss of

Oscar,

And the loss of Mikey Double L,

and of the Toby who Toby used to be.

She cried for the loss of

the dogs, who belonged to other people,

and for

the loss of Oscar again.

She cried too for the near impossibility of

wanting someone and seeing them accurately.

She felt she had lost Oscar, just when she saw him clearly,
and that she had never seen Mikey clearly,
and never would.

She felt nothing about Jack, of course, because in this possible world, he came and went, never leaving a mark.

Later, she walked to the café with the light wood floors and got an iced latte. She sat inside and texted her dog owners.

Did they want Adelaide to walk their pets during the school year? With the course schedule she had, she could do a midday walk every weekday.

She waited while they texted back.

Pretzel, no thanks.

GG Pan and Voldemort, yes.

EllaBella, yes, please.

Rabbit's owner texted back when Adelaide was on her way to the school bookstore. "Rabbit is in search of a new home. After much thought, I have decided I cannot live with a biting dog. Also, my house smells of urine. Please tell me if anyone you know might want to take her."

Yes, thought Adelaide. *I do.*

She wanted Rabbit. True, Rabbit was grumpy. And true, Rabbit had bitten her.

But Rabbit's fur was so sleek and soft. Her stocky legs were hilarious. Adelaide was fond of the way Rabbit breathed when a treat was coming out of someone's pocket. And the way she slept, with her tummy exposed.

The dog had been so sorry. She would never bite again. She deserved forgiveness.

She had already been forgiven.

Adelaide texted the owner. "We'll take her."

Then she called Levi and explained that Rabbit would be coming to live with him. "You need company," she told him. "You're sad without Mom."

"That might be true," he said.

"You're lonely."

"Also true," he said. "But why is a pit bull the solution?"

"She can wear this fabric muzzle that she has, when you're first getting to know her," Adelaide explained. "I'll walk her for you in the middle of the day."

"I can't believe you adopted me a dog," Levi said.

But he didn't sound angry.

They drove together to the store to buy rawhide bones and food. Levi texted with Rabbit's owner to get details. Then they collected Rabbit. She came with a dog bed, two bowls, and a leash.

The owner insisted on seeing Adelaide's scar, where Rabbit's teeth had gone in. "I felt safe when I got a pit bull," she said. "I thought she'd protect the house. But honestly, she never barks when anyone comes to the door, and now I'm scared she'll bite me. I've been closing her out of the bedroom."

Levi followed Adelaide's instructions and bent down low to meet Rabbit, holding out his hand. Rabbit wore her muzzle and sniffed his fingers. Then she butted her head up against his hand to be petted, briefly. *Your dad smells like a good person,* she said to Adelaide.

"You'll be really helping him out," Adelaide told Rabbit. "He needs company."

I feel bad that she doesn't want me anymore. I thought she loved me.

"We will love you," said Adelaide.

They walked Rabbit through the neighborhood and back to the house. They put her worn plaid dog bed on the floor of Levi's office. They took off the muzzle to give her water and an unscheduled meal, to make her feel at home. Levi made a call about getting his tiny backyard fenced in. They stroked Rabbit's wide silvery back and told her they would take care of her.

Stacey S drove back to campus the next morning and insisted Adelaide meet her at the café before she even unpacked her car.

"I need a double-shot latte with caramel syrup," she said. "I had so many green smoothies this summer. I am dying for caffeination. Also, I'm done with Camilla. I need to move on."

"What does that mean?" asked Adelaide as they waited in line to order coffee. " 'Moving on.' "

"I have no idea," said Stacey. "But it went sour with her at the end. Toxic, toxic."

"What flavor of toxic?"

"Camilla plays head games. Like, she tried to make me jealous. On purpose. What kind of person does that?"

"Terrible. A terrible person."

"Well, a very insecure person, anyway. And kind of mean."

They placed their orders. "How was the Toby visit?" asked Stacey.

"He's a surprisingly bossy filmmaker," said Adelaide. "And he smoked me at like, six different board games."

"So he's good."

"Yeah," said Adelaide. "It's one day at a time, but he's good."

"I saw Mikey Double L standing in front of the dining hall," said Stacey. "I wanted to snub him but I was in my car."

"Ugh. I wish I didn't have to see him. Ever. Or Aldrich. Or any of their friends. My ideal situation would be for all of them to magically not go to this stupid school anymore."

"Exhibit maximum dignity," said Stacey. "Just say, *Hey there, Mikey*, slightly condescending. And nothing more. Using *there* is important, I think. *Hey there*."

Their orders came up. They walked through campus. Adelaide saw Stacey's new room. They hung posters and made Stacey's bed. Then they went out on the balcony of Stacey's dorm. Leaning over the second-floor railing, they looked down on people moving in, lugging suitcases and laundry bags.

Cars were lined up in front of the buildings. Parents bustled around them, unloading teddy bears and speakers, cardboard boxes of books. They made piles on the stone paths and the steps. A bus from the airport pulled up and a line of students poured out, most of them dragging wheelie bags.

A disaffected boy in slouchy jeans drank a Coke on the steps.

Some guys from the basketball team jogged by wearing their jerseys.

Two girls with spiraling hair extensions and shining lips shouted when they saw each other.

A group of mousy girls came back from the student center carrying a large bag of french fries. They sat on the lawn to eat them.

Adelaide was glad to be at Alabaster. She would take sculpture and puppetry classes. There, she'd build
shapes that were
not what they seemed to be;
images of boys who were
not who they seemed to be, or who they
used to be;
images of battles that were reunions, and
whales and wool hats and tampons that stood for love. She'd build
spaces that existed only in her imagination,
contradictory rooms and
things she could not express with words,
because they would not cohere into a single, orderly story.

These things would become tangible under her fingers. And in making them, Adelaide would
heal her bleeding wounds and
release her fury; she'd
open her lungs so that she could breathe deeply the wet air of a New England fall, and she'd
open her heart to people (and dogs). She would
love herself, even with her
sadness and her
distractibility, her
defenses and her
failures.

The process of making would
stretch open the universe
until it was
frighteningly and
gloriously
wide with possibility.

Author's Note

Partial inspiration for *Again Again* comes from a short story I wrote some years ago called "How I Wrote to Toby," published in *21 Proms*. The characters' personalities and circumstances are different from what's in that original story—and that story has no alternate possible worlds in it—but that's how it went. *Constellations* by Nick Payne was another source for this novel. It is a wonderful multiverse love story.

Alabaster Preparatory Academy appears (and is interrogated, as promised) in my novel *The Disreputable History of Frankie Landau-Banks*. Luigi's pizza place can be found in that book as well.

The Factory is based loosely on Mass MOCA, the Massachusetts Museum of Contemporary Art, in North Adams. You can see images of some of the Mass MOCA exhibits mentioned below on the institution's website.

The art Adelaide sees and does is all invented by me—but with definite debts of inspiration to the following: *Half-Truths* by Paul Ramírez Jonas, at the New Museum in New York City, 2017; *The Flat Side of the Knife* by Samara Golden at MoMA

PS1, 2014; the book *Mark Dion: Contemporary Artist* by Mark Dion, Lisa Graziose Currin, Miwon Kwon, and Norman Bryson; *Garden of Eden on Wheels*, a long-term installation, and pretty much every other exhibit at the Museum of Jurassic Technology in Culver City, California; *Mary Corse: A Survey in Light* at the Whitney Museum of American Art in New York City, 2018; and the Lego art of Nathan Sawaya and Dante Dentoni (among others). Professor Byrd's print is by Kehinde Wiley. My thoughts on *Fool for Love* are influenced by Daniel Aukin's 2015 production at Manhattan Theater Club's Samuel J. Friedman Theatre, with set design by Dane Laffrey.

Acknowledgments

Many thanks to my editor, Beverly Horowitz, who gently forced me to rethink the novel completely, several times, asking all the right questions in her Beverly way. Thank you to Lauren Myracle, Gayle Forman, Daniel Aukin, and Sarah Mlynowski for reading drafts of the novel and critiquing them, and to Len Jenkin, Libba Bray, and GF for talking through plot points with me. Bob was endlessly supportive. My agent, Elizabeth Kaplan, did all the agency things but also retained faith in this book when it was really flailing. A number of dear friends whose loved ones have suffered from opioid addictions shared their family stories with me and helped me shape the emotional arcs of the novel.

At Random House, my gratitude to the whole amazing team, including but not limited to Mary McCue, Colleen Fellingham, John Adamo, Dominique Cimina, Kathleen Dunn, Rebecca Gudelis, Christine Labov, Barbara Marcus, and Adrienne Waintraub. Thanks to Jane Harris and Emma Matthewson at Hot Key Books for their early enthusiasm and support.

Thanks to Josh Pugh for supporting the charity Day One,

Voices Against Violence. For his contribution to the cause, he got to name a character: Stacey Shurman.

In early 2018, two of my students at Hamline University wrote essays that influenced my thinking on this book. I'm grateful to Miguel Camnitzer, whose research paper challenged the predominance of the monogamy paradigm in recent young adult fiction, and to Jonathan Hillman, whose paper called out the rigid beauty standards to which male characters adhere in many contemporary novels.

Ivy, Daniel, Hazel, Clementine, and Blizzard were the absolute best of the best in any possible universe.

About the Author

E. Lockhart wrote the *New York Times* bestsellers *We Were Liars* and *Genuine Fraud*. Her other books include *Fly on the Wall*, *Dramarama*, *The Disreputable History of Frankie Landau-Banks*, and the Ruby Oliver Quartet: *The Boyfriend List*, *The Boy Book*, *The Treasure Map of Boys*, and *Real Live Boyfriends*.

emilylockhart.com

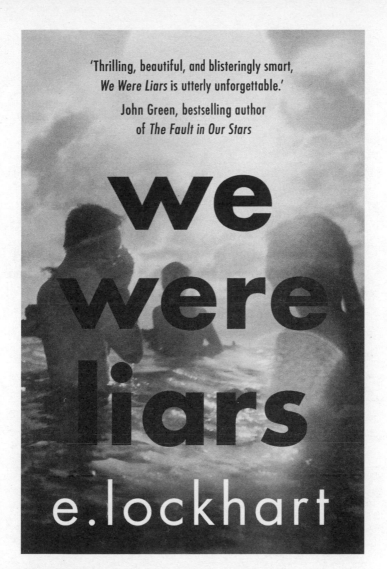

'Thrilling, beautiful, and blisteringly smart,
We Were Liars is utterly unforgettable.'

John Green, bestselling author
of *The Fault in Our Stars*

we were liars

e.lockhart

Turn the page to read an extract
from e. lockhart's bestselling
We Were Liars . . .

1

WELCOME TO THE beautiful Sinclair family.

No one is a criminal.

No one is an addict.

No one is a failure.

The Sinclairs are athletic, tall, and handsome. We are old-money Democrats. Our smiles are wide, our chins square, and our tennis serves aggressive.

It doesn't matter if divorce shreds the muscles of our hearts so that they will hardly beat without a struggle. It doesn't matter if trust-fund money is running out; if credit card bills go unpaid on the kitchen counter. It doesn't matter if there's a cluster of pill bottles on the bedside table.

It doesn't matter if one of us is desperately, desperately in love.

So much

in love

that equally desperate measures

must be taken.

We are Sinclairs.

No one is needy.

No one is wrong.

We live, at least in the summertime, on a private island off the coast of Massachusetts.

Perhaps that is all you need to know.

2

MY FULL NAME is Cadence Sinclair Eastman.

I live in Burlington, Vermont, with Mummy and three dogs.

I am nearly eighteen.

I own a well-used library card and not much else, though it is true I live in a grand house full of expensive, useless objects.

I used to be blond, but now my hair is black.

I used to be strong, but now I am weak.

I used to be pretty, but now I look sick.

It is true I suffer migraines since my accident.

It is true I do not suffer fools.

I like a twist of meaning. You see? *Suffer* migraines. Do not *suffer* fools. The word means almost the same as it did in the previous sentence, but not quite.

Suffer.

You could say it means endure, but that's not exactly right.

MY STORY STARTS before the accident. June of the summer I was fifteen, my father ran off with some woman he loved more than us.

Dad was a middling-successful professor of military history. Back then I adored him. He wore tweed jackets. He was gaunt. He drank milky tea. He was fond of board games and let me win, fond of boats and taught me to kayak, fond of bicycles, books, and art museums.

He was never fond of dogs, and it was a sign of how much he loved my mother that he let our golden retrievers sleep on the sofas and walked them three miles every morning. He was never fond of my grandparents, either, and it was a sign of how much he loved both me and Mummy that he spent every summer in Windemere House on Beechwood Island, writing articles on wars fought long ago and putting on a smile for the relatives at every meal.

That June, summer fifteen, Dad announced he was leaving and departed two days later. He told my mother he wasn't a Sinclair, and couldn't try to be one, any longer. He couldn't smile, couldn't lie, couldn't be part of that beautiful family in those beautiful houses.

Couldn't. Couldn't. Wouldn't.

He had hired moving vans already. He'd rented a house, too. My father put a last suitcase into the backseat of the Mercedes (he was leaving Mummy with only the Saab), and started the engine.

Then he pulled out a handgun and shot me in the chest. I was standing on the lawn and I fell. The bullet hole opened wide and my heart rolled out of my rib cage and down into a flower bed. Blood gushed rhythmically from my open wound,

then from my eyes,

my ears,

my mouth.

It tasted like salt and failure. The bright red shame of being unloved soaked the grass in front of our house, the bricks of the path, the steps to the porch. My heart spasmed among the peonies like a trout.

Mummy snapped. She said to get hold of myself.

Be normal, now, she said. Right now, she said.

Because you are. Because you can be.

Don't cause a scene, she told me. Breathe and sit up.

I did what she asked.

She was all I had left.

Mummy and I tilted our square chins high as Dad drove down the hill. Then we went indoors and trashed the gifts he'd given us: jewelry, clothes, books, anything. In the days that followed, we got rid of the couch and armchairs my parents had bought together. Tossed the wedding china, the silver, the photographs.

We purchased new furniture. Hired a decorator. Placed an order for Tiffany silverware. Spent a day walking through art galleries and bought paintings to cover the empty spaces on our walls.

We asked Granddad's lawyers to secure Mummy's assets.

Then we packed our bags and went to Beechwood Island.

3

PENNY, CARRIE, AND Bess are the daughters of Tipper and Harris Sinclair. Harris came into his money at twenty-one after Harvard and grew the fortune doing business I never bothered to understand. He inherited houses and land. He made intelligent decisions about the stock market. He married Tipper and kept her in the kitchen and the garden. He put her on display in pearls and on sailboats. She seemed to enjoy it.

Granddad's only failure was that he never had a son, but no matter. The Sinclair daughters were sunburnt and blessed. Tall, merry, and rich, those girls were like princesses in a fairy tale. They were known throughout Boston, Harvard Yard, and Martha's Vineyard for their cashmere cardigans and grand parties. They were made for legends. Made for princes and Ivy League schools, ivory statues and majestic houses.

Granddad and Tipper loved the girls so, they couldn't say whom they loved best. First Carrie, then Penny, then Bess, then Carrie again. There were splashy weddings with salmon and harpists, then bright blond grandchildren and funny blond dogs. No one could ever have been prouder of their beautiful American girls than Tipper and Harris were, back then.

They built three new houses on their craggy private island and gave them each a name: Windemere for Penny, Red Gate for Carrie, and Cuddledown for Bess.

I am the eldest Sinclair grandchild. Heiress to the island, the fortune, and the expectations.

Well, probably.

4

ME, JOHNNY, MIRREN, and Gat. Gat, Mirren, Johnny, and me.

The family calls us four the Liars, and probably we deserve it. We are all nearly the same age, and we all have birthdays in the fall. Most years on the island, we've been trouble.

Gat started coming to Beechwood the year we were eight. Summer eight, we called it.

Before that, Mirren, Johnny, and I weren't Liars. We were

nothing but cousins, and Johnny was a pain because he didn't like playing with girls.

Johnny, he is bounce, effort, and snark. Back then he would hang our Barbies by the necks or shoot us with guns made of Lego.

Mirren, she is sugar, curiosity, and rain. Back then she spent long afternoons with Taft and the twins, splashing at the big beach, while I drew pictures on graph paper and read in the hammock on the Clairmont house porch.

Then Gat came to spend the summers with us.

Aunt Carrie's husband left her when she was pregnant with Johnny's brother, Will. I don't know what happened. The family never speaks of it. By summer eight, Will was a baby and Carrie had taken up with Ed already.

This Ed, he was an art dealer and he adored the kids. That was all we'd heard about him when Carrie announced she was bringing him to Beechwood, along with Johnny and the baby.

They were the last to arrive that summer, and most of us were on the dock waiting for the boat to pull in. Granddad lifted me up so I could wave at Johnny, who was wearing an orange life vest and shouting over the prow.

Granny Tipper stood next to us. She turned away from the boat for a moment, reached in her pocket, and brought out a white peppermint. Unwrapped it and tucked it into my mouth.

As she looked back at the boat, Gran's face changed. I squinted to see what she saw.

Carrie stepped off with Will on her hip. He was in a baby's yellow life vest, and was really no more than a shock of white-blond hair sticking up over it. A cheer went up at the sight of him. That vest, which we had all worn as babies. The hair. How wonderful that this little boy we didn't know yet was so obviously a Sinclair.

Johnny leapt off the boat and threw his own vest on the dock. First thing, he ran up to Mirren and kicked her. Then he kicked me. Kicked the twins. Walked over to our grandparents and stood up straight. "Good to see you, Granny and Granddad. I look forward to a happy summer."

Tipper hugged him. "Your mother told you to say that, didn't she?"

"Yes," said Johnny. "And I'm to say, nice to see you again."

"Good boy."

"Can I go now?"

Tipper kissed his freckled cheek. "Go on, then."

Ed followed Johnny, having stopped to help the staff unload the luggage from the motorboat. He was tall and slim. His skin was very dark: Indian heritage, we'd later learn. He wore black-framed glasses and was dressed in dapper city clothes: a linen suit and striped shirt. The pants were wrinkled from traveling.

Granddad set me down.

Granny Tipper's mouth made a straight line. Then she showed all her teeth and went forward.

"You must be Ed. What a lovely surprise."

He shook hands. "Didn't Carrie tell you we were coming?"

"Of course she did."

Ed looked around at our white, white family. Turned to Carrie. "Where's Gat?"

They called for him, and he climbed from the inside of the boat, taking off his life vest, looking down to undo the buckles.

"Mother, Dad," said Carrie, "we brought Ed's nephew to play with Johnny. This is Gat Patil."

Granddad reached out and patted Gat's head. "Hello, young man."

"Hello."

"His father passed on, just this year," explained Carrie. "He and Johnny are the best of friends. It's a big help to Ed's sister if we take him for a few weeks. And, Gat? You'll get to have cookouts and go swimming like we talked about. Okay?"

But Gat didn't answer. He was looking at me.

His nose was dramatic, his mouth sweet. Skin deep brown, hair black and waving. Body wired with energy. Gat seemed spring-loaded. Like he was searching for something. He was contemplation and enthusiasm. Ambition and strong coffee. I could have looked at him forever.

Our eyes locked.

I turned and ran away.

Gat followed. I could hear his feet behind me on the wooden walkways that cross the island.

I kept running. He kept following.

Johnny chased Gat. And Mirren chased Johnny.

The adults remained talking on the dock, circling politely around Ed, cooing over baby Will. The littles did whatever littles do.

We four stopped running at the tiny beach down by Cuddledown House. It's a small stretch of sand with high rocks on either side. No one used it much, back then. The big beach had softer sand and less seaweed.

Mirren took off her shoes and the rest of us followed. We tossed stones into the water. We just existed.

I wrote our names in the sand.

Cadence, Mirren, Johnny, and Gat.

Gat, Johnny, Mirren, and Cadence.

That was the beginning of us.

* * *

JOHNNY BEGGED TO have Gat stay longer.

He got what he wanted.

The next year he begged to have him come for the entire summer.

Gat came.

Johnny was the first grandson. My grandparents almost never said no to Johnny.

5

SUMMER FOURTEEN, GAT and I took out the small motorboat alone. It was just after breakfast. Bess made Mirren play tennis with the twins and Taft. Johnny had started running that year and was doing loops around the perimeter path. Gat found me in the Clairmont kitchen and asked, did I want to take the boat out?

"Not really." I wanted to go back to bed with a book.

"Please?" Gat almost never said please.

"Take it out yourself."

"I can't borrow it," he said. "I don't feel right."

"Of course you can borrow it."

"Not without one of you."

He was being ridiculous. "Where do you want to go?" I asked.

"I just want to get off-island. Sometimes I can't stand it here."

I couldn't imagine, then, what it was he couldn't stand, but I said all right. We motored out to sea in wind jackets and bathing suits. After a bit, Gat cut the engine. We sat eating pistachios and breathing salt air. The sunlight shone on the water.

"Let's go in," I said.

Gat jumped and I followed, but the water was so much colder than off the beach, it snatched our breath. The sun went behind a cloud. We laughed panicky laughs and shouted that it was the stupidest idea to get in the water. What had we been thinking? There were sharks off the coast, everybody knew that.

Don't talk about sharks, God! We scrambled and pushed each other, struggling to be the first one up the ladder at the back of the boat.

After a minute, Gat leaned back and let me go first. "Not because you're a girl but because I'm a good person," he told me.

"Thanks." I stuck out my tongue.

"But when a shark bites my legs off, promise to write a speech about how awesome I was."

"Done," I said. "Gatwick Matthew Patil made a delicious meal."

It seemed hysterically funny to be so cold. We didn't have towels. We huddled together under a fleece blanket we found under the seats, our bare shoulders touching each other. Cold feet, on top of one another.

"This is only so we don't get hypothermia," said Gat. "Don't think I find you pretty or anything."

"I know you don't."

"You're hogging the blanket."

"Sorry."

A pause.

Gat said, "I do find you pretty, Cady. I didn't mean that the way it came out. In fact, when did you get so pretty? It's distracting."

"I look the same as always."

"You changed over the school year. It's putting me off my game."

"You have a game?"

He nodded solemnly.

"That is the dumbest thing I ever heard. What is your game?"

"Nothing penetrates my armor. Hadn't you noticed?"

That made me laugh. "No."

"Damn. I thought it was working."

We changed the subject. Talked about bringing the littles to Edgartown to see a movie in the afternoon, about sharks and whether they really ate people, about *Plants Versus Zombies*.

Then we drove back to the island.

Not long after that, Gat started lending me his books and finding me at the tiny beach in the early evenings. He'd search me out when I was lying on the Windemere lawn with the goldens.

We started walking together on the path that circles the island, Gat in front and me behind. We'd talk about books or invent imaginary worlds. Sometimes we'd end up walking several times around the edge before we got hungry or bored.

Beach roses lined the path, deep pink. Their smell was faint and sweet.

One day I looked at Gat, lying in the Clairmont hammock with a book, and he seemed, well, like he was mine. Like he was my particular person.

I got in the hammock next to him, silently. I took the pen

out of his hand—he always read with a pen—and wrote *Gat* on the back of his left, and *Cadence* on the back of his right.

He took the pen from me. Wrote *Gat* on the back of my left, and *Cadence* on the back of my right.

I am not talking about fate. I don't believe in destiny or soul mates or the supernatural. I just mean we understood each other. All the way.

But we were only fourteen. I had never kissed a boy, though I would kiss a few the next school year, and somehow we didn't label it love.

Praise for
We Were Liars

'Thrilling, beautiful, and blisteringly smart,
We Were Liars is utterly unforgettable.'
– John Green, #1 New York Times bestselling
author of *The Fault in Our Stars*

'Irresistible' – *New York Times*

'Bowl-you-over' – *Cosmopolitan*

'So freaking good' – Sarah Dessen

'Such beautiful writing' – Libba Bray

'Beautiful and disturbing' – Justine Larbalestier

'Better than the hype' – Lauren Oliver

'Haunting, sophisticated' – *Wall Street Journal*

'A cunning, clever and **absolutely gripping** novel, full of surprises, which sent me straight back to its first page as soon as I reached the last.' – *Guardian*

'**You're going to want to remember the title**. Liars details the summers of a girl who harbors a dark secret, and delivers a satisfying but shocking twist ending.' – Breia Brissey, *Entertainment Weekly*

'Riveting, brutal and **beautifully told**.' – *Kirkus Reviews*

'**Surprising, thrilling, and beautifully executed** in spare, precise, and lyrical prose. Lockhart spins a tragic family drama, the roots of which go back generations. And the ending? Shhhh. Not telling. (But it's a doozy.) . . . This is poised to be big.' – *Booklist*, starred review

'A haunting tale about how families live within their own mythologies. **Sad, wonderful, and real**.' – Scott Westerfeld, author of *Uglies* and *Leviathan*

'**Spectacular**.' – Lauren Myracle, author of *Shine*, *The Infinite Moment of Us*, and *TTYL*

'A haunting, brilliant, beautiful book. **This is E. Lockhart at her mind-blowing best**.' – Sarah Mlynowski, author of *Don't Even Think About It* and *Gimme a Call*

'Dark, gripping, heartrending, and **terrifyingly smart**, this book grabs you from the first page – and will never let go.' – Robin Wasserman, author of *The Waking Dark*

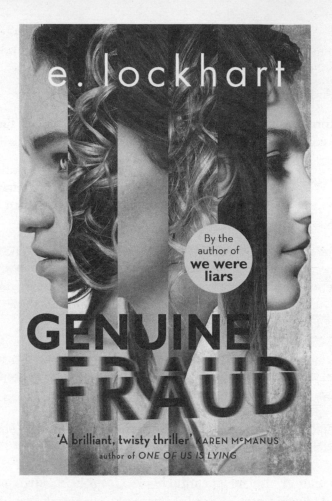

e. lockhart

By the
author of
**we were
liars**

GENUINE
FRAUD

'A brilliant, twisty thriller' KAREN MᶜMANUS
author of *ONE OF US IS LYING*

'An addictive and shocking feminist thriller.'
– Lena Dunham

'A brilliant, twisty thriller – I loved it!'
– Karen M. McManus, bestselling author of
One of Us Is Lying

'Compulsively readable.' – *Entertainment Weekly*

'This thriller from the author of *We Were Liars* will **challenge preconceptions** about identity and keep readers guessing' – *Kirkus Reviews*

'An unsettling but **thoroughly satisfying** read' – *Buzzfeed*

'A thriller that will leave you shook from start to finish' – *Maximum Pop*

'A rollercoaster of a mystery novel by the author who brought you We Were Liars. If you like your novels full of **intrigue, suspense, and completely unpredictable plot twists** then this book is definitely for you' – *The Book Bag*

'Plays on the desire to reinvent yourself, to gain a fortune and live a carefree life. Its protagonist **will stay in your memory** long after you have finished the story' – *Armadillo Magazine*

'An update of *The Talented Mr Ripley*, told in trendy reverse chronology' – *Financial Times*

'A noir thriller **full of glamour and suspense** that will keep twisting you up in knots . . . the two strong female characters will keep you guessing until the end.' – *South Wales Evening Post*

'A **sophisticated, emotionally literate** whodunit . . . As well as a mystery to solve, there's human need and insecurity to contemplate' – *Observer*

'Nail-bitingly tense, this exploration of identity, entitlement and feminism is **a perfect psychological thriller** and surely, soon, a movie' – *Daily Mail*

'*Genuine Fraud* is a disquieting book, one built craftily enough to reward repeat readings' – *New York Times*

'It's hard to see how E. Lockhart could surpass the bestselling *We Were Liars* but this release is another psychological suspense novel' – *U Magazine*

'I want to tell the whole world about it. It's **INCREDIBLE**' – Hannah Witt

Thank you for choosing a Hot Key book.

If you want to know more about our authors
and what we publish, you can find us online.

You can start at our website

www.hotkeybooks.com

And you can also find us on:

We hope to see you soon!